GODWIN'S GROCERY

SWEET TEA AND A SOUTHERN GENTLEMAN
BOOK 4

ANNE-MARIE MEYER

"You want me to kiss you, Claire?"

JAX

ANNE-MARIE MEYER

GODWIN'S GROCERY

SWEET TEA &
SOUTHERN GENTLEMAN

4

To those who believe in second chances.

CLAIRE

SWEET TEA &
SOUTHERN GENTLEMAN

Senior Year

"You're so lucky," my best friend, Kelly, said as she stretched out on my bed. Her head hung off one side, so she could stare at me. She gave me a mock-jealous stare before she closed her eyes and pretended to hug herself. "Jax and I are soulmates. Jax and I are going to get married." She slit her eyes and frowned at me. "It's gross."

I laughed as I swiveled back to my vanity mirror and picked up a makeup brush to finish smoothing out my blush. "You'll find your Romeo someday," I said and then felt bad. No matter how nicely I said those words, they always came out sounding condescending even if I meant them in a supportive way.

"You'll find your Romeo someday," she mocked as she pushed herself up to sitting and then grabbed my penguin stuffed animal that Jax won me at the county fair last summer and hugged it to her chest. "It's just not fair that you found yours in high school. I'm going to have to go slogging through men in college to find him." She blew her hair away from her face. "Some people have all the luck."

I waved away her words as I smeared on some lip gloss. "He's out there. You just have to wait until he shows up." I blotted my lips a few times before I turned to face her. "He will show up." My voice had turned firm. I hated that my best friend wanted nothing more than to fall in love.

If I could, I'd will her Prince Charming into existence. I loved Kelly, but her sour attitude took my happiness down sometimes. I just wished we could both be in a relationship, so we could both be happy.

I stood and walked over to my closet, where I turned on the light and began to skim the shirts that were hanging up. I wanted to look done up. It was our six-month anniversary, and I wanted to look special.

It had been six months since we finally admitted we had feelings for each other after fighting the whole summer while working at Harmony Megaplex together. Six months since he first kissed me behind the movie theater. And six months that I'd been able to keep our relationship a secret from my family.

I never really understood why the Hodges family hated the Robinsons. Something to do with a land dispute decades ago. For as long as I'd been alive, we weren't allowed to associate with anyone from the Robinson family. So for me to fall head over heels in love with Jax was just asking for a tornado to whip through my happiness before demanding that I never speak to him again.

Which is why we had a plan. We could keep our relationship a secret. There were only a few more months before we graduated, and then Jax and I could run away from this small town and never look back. We could live in happiness forever, away from our toxic families and their ridiculous grudge.

In just a few months, I would be free.

"I was thinking this black shirt," I said as I pulled it off the hanger and held it up for Kelly to see.

Before she could respond, there was a knock on my door. Panic filled my chest, and Kelly must have understood as well because her eyes widened as she stared at me. I swallowed my nerves as I set the shirt on the top of my dresser and headed over to the door.

Mom was standing on the other side. She looked pale, and her eyes were dark as she stared at me. She took her time inspecting my face before she met my gaze. "Going somewhere?"

I shifted my weight and nodded, waving toward Kelly, who was now standing next to my bed. "Kelly and I are going to go hang out with some people from school."

Mom flicked her gaze to Kelly before she glanced back down at me. "Can I talk to you in the hallway for a moment?"

I glanced back at Kelly, who gave me an encouraging

smile, before I nodded and joined my mom in the hallway. She shut the door and then turned to face me.

"I need to tell you something," she whispered.

She wasn't angry. She wasn't upset. She was...sad. And it was disarming.

"Okay," I said, drawing the word out.

She moved away from the door to lean against the wall. She folded her arms, her gaze never leaving my face. "Your father is leaving us."

My stomach dropped to the floor. It felt as if all of the blood in my body went with it. I blinked, trying to process her words. "What?"

Mom sighed as she unfolded her arms and pinched the bridge of her nose. "He's been unhappy for a long time. Today, he told me that he has no intention of coming back."

Tears were forming on my eyelids. I blinked a few times, hoping that it would dispel them. I didn't want to have to redo my makeup. If what Mom said was true, the last thing I wanted was to stay in this house with my mother and the memories haunting the hallways.

"What about m..." My voice drifted off at the same rate that Mom's eyebrows rose.

She knew what I was trying to say before the words even left my lips.

"What about you?" she asked.

I pinched my lips together and nodded. I knew my parents weren't happy. They barely spoke. Dad had been going on week-long "business trips." I doubted he even went anywhere —he just chose to sleep in his office over being here with Mom. Even with all of that, he always made time for me. He'd text or call, and when he would come back to the house after his long "trips," he'd take me to the movies or to get dinner.

So, the fact that he was just packing up and leaving without even telling me was strange.

Mom shrugged. "I guess he's wanting to start over. He has a new girlfriend, and he wants a new family with her." Mom's tone was so harsh that it felt as if she had smacked me even though she hadn't moved from her spot.

"A girlfriend?" was all I could muster.

"Yes. Your father has been cheating on me."

I took a step back. The air around me was rapidly being sucked away, and I felt as if I were suffocating. I needed fresh air. I needed to get away from my mother and the sharpness of her words. I wanted her to stop, but she didn't look as if she was going to anytime soon.

"Of course, the floozy your father chose to cheat on me with was someone he knew would hurt me more than anything." Mom massaged her temples with her forefingers. "Out of all the women in town, why did it have to be Camilla Robinson?"

My heart stopped beating. My entire body went cold. I stared at Mom, wondering if I had just hallucinated or if she had really said those words. "Camilla Robinson?"

Mom's gaze snapped to mine. She narrowed her eyes as

if she knew I wasn't telling her something. "What do you know?"

Tears were flowing now. I shook my head. I couldn't say anything, even if I wanted to. My heart felt as if it were bleeding inside of me, and there was nothing I could do to stop it. I turned away from her in an effort to compose myself, but Mom wasn't having it. She grabbed my shoulder and turned me back around so that I was facing her.

"Claire, you need to tell me. If you've had any contact with a Robinson, you need to cut it off. Of course, a Robinson would stop at nothing to embarrass this family. Even seduce the people close to me just to punish me." She had both hands on my shoulders now, so I couldn't turn away.

The only thing I could do was stare at her as her gaze bored into mine. And then understanding passed across her face as she dropped her hands and stepped back. "You have a thing with their younger son. Jax?"

Just at the mention of his name, a sob escaped my lips. I slapped my hand to my mouth in an effort to stifle it. Mom's eyes narrowed. She didn't need me to say anything. She'd already gotten her answer.

"You must never see him again. He wants nothing more than to embarrass this family. He is using you just like his mother is using your father." Mom dipped down to catch my gaze.

I was so emotionally exhausted that all I could do was

hold her gaze. I needed someone to tell me what to do. There was no way my brain could think for itself.

"Dump him. Dump him, Claire. Don't let a Robinson ruin this family any more. If he told you that he loved you, then he lied. You need to walk away before a Robinson causes any more damage to us."

I slowly began to nod. Did Jax know about this? Had he been leading me on this whole time? It hadn't felt like a lie. The way he held me. The way he kissed me. The way he told me that I was all he ever wanted. That had felt real. Our families hated each other, but it didn't matter. He was the person I was born to love.

Had that all been a lie? Was he so wrapped up in this family feud that he would get a job where I was working, seduce me, and make me fall in love with him, only to drop me once I was fully hooked? Did he not know that his mom was cheating with my dad?

Had they been working together?

Mom took a step toward me, startling me from my thoughts. I took a step back, but Mom was faster. She wrapped her arms around my shoulders and pulled me into a hug. I could count on one hand the number of times Mom had hugged me. My entire body stiffened as she held me and patted my head.

"I know it hurts. But it's for the best. It's better to walk away now than let this relationship linger." She pulled back and glanced down at me.

My eyes were puffy, and my nose was running. I sniffled, and Mom took a step back.

"Promise me that you'll break up with Jax?"

I wiped my nose with my sleeve and nodded. A look of relief passed over Mom's face. "Good." Then she patted me on the back and opened my bedroom door. "I've got a pizza coming. Why don't you get dressed in some pajamas, and you and Kelly can watch a movie. I'll bring the food up as soon as it's here."

I moved toward my open door, my body completely numb. I couldn't feel my feet on the ground, but I knew that I was walking. Once I was inside my room, Mom shut the door behind me. Kelly came over. Her eyebrows were drawn together, and she was studying me.

"What happened?" she asked, her voice full of concern.

Another sob escaped, and my entire body collapsed onto my bed. I buried my face into my comforter as I mumbled, "I have to break up with Jax."

"What?" Kelly asked, the mattress shifting as she joined me on the bed.

I tipped my face to the side, not caring that my makeup was ruined. I was certain I looked like a raccoon left out in the rain too long. I wasn't going anywhere tonight. In fact, I was done with boys until I got out of this god-forsaken town. The only men I was going to allow myself to think about were the guys in my books.

Real guys just ripped out your heart and stomped on it.

I took in a deep breath, steeled my emotions as I met her gaze, and said, "Jax and I are finished."

1

CLAIRE

SWEET TEA & SOUTHERN GENTLEMAN

The blare of my alarm caused me to moan and pull my pillow over my face. It was 5 a.m. on a Tuesday, and if I didn't get out of bed and get Carmel out for her walk, Mom would be up and getting breakfast started, and I'd miss my window to slip out before she saw me.

But I was so tired. It felt like a monumental task to pull my body out of bed and get dressed.

"Blast you, dog," I murmured as I rubbed my eyes and yanked my comforter off my body. I stretched my arms over my head and yawned as I tried to loosen my stiff muscles.

Mom had gone on a rampage yesterday, and we spent the whole day stripping beds and vacuuming mattresses. There was a huge fishing competition this weekend, and she was booked solid. I could tell the idea of being fully booked had her anxiety spiking above the normally elevated level. I thought about talking to her about it, but decided against it.

After all, it was a miracle our relationship hadn't gotten worse with me being here. I wasn't going to push my luck.

I shook my body to help my muscles wake up and stood. I slipped out of my pajamas and into a pair of yoga pants and a tank. I tied my tennis shoes, and on my way out of my room, I grabbed my old hoodie and pulled it over my head.

I paused once I was in the hallway and tipped my head to the side, trying to catch any sign of life in the house. The only noise that reached my ears was the rhythmic ticking of the grandfather clock in the foyer that my mother had inherited from her mother.

I sighed and made my way to the kitchen, where I grabbed a glass of water before pushing through the back door out to the porch. I bounded down the steps and glanced around one more time before I made my way to the shed. I could hear Carmel whining as I neared.

I hated that I had to keep her here, but it was the only option. I hadn't come clean with Mom, and I feared what she would say if she found out. Sally, my ex-roommate had called to tell me she had taken a job in St. Louis, so I needed to find a different apartment. She'd boxed up my stuff and rented a storage unit for me.

My job had called to say that they would have to take me off payroll if I didn't tell them definitively when I was going to return. I told them I'd be back after this weekend, which seemed to appease them. Mom was getting better, and with Rose here, I was just getting in the way.

"Carmel," I whispered. Her nose appeared between the door and the frame as soon as I started to push inside. Her tail was wagging, shaking her now round belly.

She found my hand and started licking it over and over. I laughed as I crouched down and scratched behind both of her ears. She turned her attention to my nose, and I let her lick me a few times before I stood and reached for the leash I'd stashed on a hook in the back.

"Come on, girl." I hooked the leash to her collar and turned back to open the door. "Let's get you out of here before someone sees you." I paused at the door and peeked out to make sure that the coast was clear.

Then, I made a kissing noise, and Carmel fell into step with me as I hurried toward the woods and slipped into the protection of the trees.

It was a beautiful morning. The smell of dew and leaves filled my nose as I walked Carmel on the now worn path we'd made in the woods behind Apple Blossom B&B. The sky was warming with the sun, whose rays were peeking over the horizon. I let my mind wander as I studied the path in front of me.

It was strange that I'd been here for a month and a half already. Time had just flown by. I guess when you're hiding a secret from your family, the days just tick by. Mom had been a bit more manageable since I'd promised to stay until she could fully return to her tasks around the B&B.

I didn't bother to tell her about losing my apartment or

Carmel. It seemed like she appreciated my help, which made my stay less strained.

Anything I could do to get through my time here, I was going to do.

We passed by the pond where I'd run into Jax, and my entire body heated from the memory. I'd managed to keep my contact with him brief and concise. After I texted him that Carmel was pregnant, he responded that he would help take care of her, which I appreciated.

He even came to the vet appointment where we found out that there were at least five puppies in there. He hadn't said much. Instead, he just kept to the far wall and let me converse with the vet. I hated the inquisitive look that the vet tech gave me as her gaze drifted from Jax to me.

Thankfully, she didn't say anything about Jax being my ex or what this meant for us. When I went to pay, Jax stepped in and handed his card over to the receptionist. If he saw my glare, he didn't comment on it. Instead, he kept his gaze forward until the receptionist handed him back his card and the receipt to sign.

Last week he stopped me on the street and insisted that I come to the pub to get the bag of dog food he'd bought for Carmel. Besides that, he kept his distance.

I hated and loved that at the same time. Being in my hometown was bringing up all of my old feelings, and I hadn't realized how stitched into my past Jax was. Every corner. Every building. Every person reminded me of Jax and the feelings I used to have for him.

It was its own kind of torture that faded but never went away.

Wailing sirens drew my attention up. I looked through the trees in the direction it was coming from but couldn't make out what department it was or where it was going.

I glanced down to see Carmel had heard as well. Her body was pointed in the direction of the sound. Her ears were lifted, and her head tipped to the side. She whimpered, so I reached down and scratched her head.

"Let's go, girl," I said as I turned to head back.

She looked tired, and I didn't want to push her farther than she wanted to go. Plus, I had this feeling in my gut that the sirens were headed in the direction of the B&B.

As we got closer, I saw the lights of an ambulance through the trees. My stomach dropped. People were gathered around, and when I saw the orange paint of Rose's Toyota Corolla in the middle of them, all thought left my mind.

I sprinted the rest of the way through the woods, across the yard, and pushed through the group. Tears filled my eyes as I stared down at Rose.

She must have collapsed as she was getting out of her car. The driver's door was open, and she was lying on the ground just outside of it. Her skin was pale, and her eyes were closed.

"Rose?" I whispered as I tried to push past an EMT to get to her.

"Ma'am," the EMT said as they lifted their hand to stop me.

Two other EMTs moved to lift Rose's body up to put her on a gurney. Her arms fell to the sides of her body, and the reality of what was happening hit me like a freight train.

"No!" I wailed, suddenly finding my voice. I pushed against the EMT's arms, which had surrounded me. "Let me go!" I screamed as I struggled to break his hold.

"Ma'am, you cannot go over there." His voice was direct and sharp as he held me against his chest.

Tears were streaming down my cheeks. This couldn't be happening. Rose was more of a mother to me than my own mother was. My mom was standing a few feet off, watching as the EMTs rolled Rose's limp body over to the ambulance.

I hated her so much. Why was she just standing there? Why wasn't she crying? Why wasn't she trying to stop what was happening? Why wasn't she being the mother I needed her to be?

"Listen, she's weak but alive. We're doing our job here. You need to calm down." The EMT's voice was gruff but kind, and it startled me.

I stopped fighting and glanced up to see his dark blue eyes staring down at me. He couldn't be much older than me with his tousled blond hair and soft smile that made the skin around his eyes crinkle. I stifled a sob and nodded.

"Are you going to let us do our job?" he asked, and I began to feel his grip on me loosen.

"Yes," I whispered.

He eyed me before he let me go and took a step back. He pushed his hand through his hair and then waved toward the ambulance. "We're taking her to Harmony Medical. You can follow us if you want to."

My entire body felt numb, and I lost the ability to speak, so I just followed his gesture with my gaze.

He studied me for a moment longer before he jogged over to the ambulance and climbed in the back. The sirens began to wail as the ambulance headed down the drive and disappeared down the main road.

The crowd that had gathered began to make their way back to the B&B. Their conversations were kept to a soft hush.

It took me a moment to find my strength. I glanced around and realized that Rose's car door was still open, so I walked over to it and wrapped my fingers around it before I stopped. Rose's purse was dumped out on the mat in front of the driver's seat. Tears began to flow once more as I crouched down and began to stuff her things back inside her familiar and well-worn brown leather purse.

Once everything was cleaned up, I held her purse to my chest as I stood and slammed the door behind me.

I startled when I was met with the dark eyes of my mother. Her lips were tipped down into a frown, and her eyebrows were drawn together as if she were mad at me.

"Ma—"

"Why is there a dog on my property?" Her voice was

low, and suddenly, I felt as if I were a child again, getting reprimanded for stealing a cookie.

"What?" I asked. Her words weren't quite registering.

"The dog. Why are you holding a leash with a dog attached to the other end?"

I shifted my left hand, and the heavy feeling of a leash wrapped around my wrist brought me back to reality. I glanced down to see Carmel standing behind my legs. Her body was shaking as if this had all been too much for her.

Realization washed over me when I returned my gaze to my mother. There was fire in her eyes now. She knew that I'd been keeping a secret from her. But what I couldn't understand was why she cared more about this than Rose being transported to the hospital?

"I've had her here since you were in the hospital. Abigail needed a place for her, and she knew I took care of animals." The story just spilled out of me. There was a sense of relief that came from finally telling the truth, and right now, I felt as if I were going to crumble under all of the emotional stress I'd been carrying around.

"Abigail? The girl that owns the bookstore?" Mom's face turned a brighter shade of red. "The one that is friends with *Shelby*?" Mom spat her name as if it tasted bad on her tongue.

"What does it matter now? I need to get to the hospital," I said as I sidestepped her and started my way back to the B&B so I could get my keys.

"Where are you going?" Mom's voice grew louder. I

knew that she was following me, but I wasn't going to stop. "You're not taking a dog into my house." Her voice had hit an octave that I hadn't heard in a long time.

Suddenly, my hand whipped back. I turned to see that Mom had yanked the leash off my wrist, and she was now holding it high in the air.

"I do not allow animals on my property." She turned on her heel and started marching a very frightened Carmel toward the main road.

"Mom!" I screamed as I ran after her. I wasn't sure what she was going to do, but I feared what she was capable of.

"I told you this when you were a child, and my position hasn't changed. I *do not* allow animals at the B&B."

I finally caught up with them. I reached down and scooped Carmel up in my arms. Anger coursed through me when I realized that she was shivering. When the leash went taut, Mom turned to face me.

"Get her off my property."

I was shaking now. I wanted to scream profanities at my mother, but I couldn't find the words. How could she be worried about Carmel when Rose was in an ambulance right now with an unknown future? Why did she always have to be so harsh?

"I'll find her another place to stay," I finally managed, my voice hoarse from the emotions that had solidified there. I turned and started making my way over to my car. I wasn't sure where I was going to bring her, but I knew I couldn't leave her here with Mom.

"Claire?"

I turned to face her. She had her arms crossed in front of her chest. Her jaw was set, and there was no emotion in her gaze. Any hope that she might actually take back her words and let Carmel stay slipped away with the morning breeze.

"Yes?" I asked.

"Find another place to stay as well."

2

JAX

SWEET TEA &
SOUTHERN GENTLEMAN

S team filled the bathroom as I climbed into the shower. The water pelted my body as I stood there, waiting for my skin to acclimate to the heat. It had been a long night last night at the bar, and I was exhausted. I didn't want to wake up, but I had a delivery scheduled for the god-awful time of eight in the morning, and Henry wasn't going to be there to sign for it.

"Some days, it sucks to be the boss," I muttered under my breath as I turned to grab my shampoo bottle. I squeezed a dollop into my hand before slathering it in my hair.

I rinsed off my hands and then leaned them against the back shower wall, letting the water rinse the soap from my hair. I closed my eyes and tipped my head forward. I felt my body relax, and a moment later, I jolted awake.

Startled, I stood up straight and pushed my hands through my hair as I looked around. I was going to fall asleep in the shower if I didn't watch myself. I grabbed my loofah and bar of soap, sudsed it up, and began scrubbing.

The faint sound of knocking caused me to pause. I glanced toward the front door, as if I had the superpower to see through walls, but then shook my head. I finished cleaning my body, but as I was rinsing off, the sound came again.

I flipped the water off and waited. Was I hearing things or was someone really at my door? I tried to dust the cobwebs off my brain and force myself to remember if anyone was coming over this early in the morning.

Aunt Pricilla.

Gramps.

Shit.

I flipped the water back on, rinsed off, and then turned the shower off. I grabbed a nearby towel, wrapped it around my waist, and sprinted to the door.

Aunt Pricilla had taken Grandpa to see my mom in South Carolina, and she was going to drop him off with me on her way to work. I'd completely forgotten.

I half ran, half slid across the hardwood floor to the front door and grabbed the handle. The rapid sound of knocking caused my anxiety to rise as I twisted the lock and pulled the door open.

"I know. I forgot—"

My entire body froze. And it seemed like Claire had the same reaction. Her puffy eyes were wide, and her lips parted as she stared at me. Then slowly—painfully slowly—her gaze drifted down my chest to the towel I was clutching around my waist.

"Claire?" I finally managed out. Out of everyone that I could think of to bother me at seven in the morning, Claire Hodges was not on my Bingo card.

She slapped her hand over her eyes and tipped her face toward the sky. "I'm so sorry. I didn't think that you would answer the door half-na..." She pinched her lips to stop the rest of the word from being spoken.

"I was just in the shower," I said as I pushed my hand through my hair, spraying water everywhere. "Which is where people normally are this early in the morning."

Her whole body stiffened.

With her protecting her eyes, I tied the towel around my waist, brushed off the water droplets still clinging to my skin, and then folded my arms. "You can look. I'm not *actually* naked."

I watched as her cheeks flushed, and I smiled. It would have bothered me if she wasn't affected by the sight of my bare chest. It would have crushed me. But blushing at the mention of my naked body? That told me that she still had feelings, whether good or bad. And that, that I could live with.

Slowly, she peeled her fingers one by one away from her eyes and then dropped her face, her gaze was the last thing she lowered. She studied me, and I suddenly realized that she was hurting.

Her puffy eyes. Her tear-stained cheeks. The cloud that

hung over her had my entire body tensing and preparing for a fight. I was ready to take out whoever had made her feel this way.

"What's wrong?" I asked before I could stop myself. I moved to step forward but then stopped and rocked back to a solid footing.

Thankfully, Claire didn't notice. Instead, she wrapped her arms around her chest and glanced around my porch. "Rose went to the hospital today."

A wave of concern washed through my body. "What?"

"She had a heart attack. They took her away by ambulance, and she's in surgery, getting a stint put in." She stared at the ground. "I was there for the last two hours, but then I had to leave..." Her voice trailed off as she glanced back to her car.

I was so confused. Claire wasn't speaking in sentences that I understood. "Do you want me to go with you to the hospital?" The breeze picked up, and I was made very aware of the fact that I was standing in the doorway wearing just a towel.

Claire glanced over at me. "No. That's not why I'm here."

I shifted my weight. "Then why are you here?"

She chewed on her bottom lip. I could tell that she didn't want to say whatever was lingering on the tip of her tongue. "My mom kicked me out of the B&B. She found Carmel and told me that I wasn't welcome back." As if she just heard her name, I saw Carmel's face appear in the back window of Claire's car.

"And since you're the reason I'm in this situation to begin with, I figured you'd be the person to help me. I can't go back to Florida. I have no place to stay, and with Rose in the hospital, I'm not leaving until I know that she's okay."

I studied Claire as she spoke, but she refused to look at me. Instead, her gaze flitted from my chest to the ground and then over to the house numbers that ran down next to my front door.

"How long do you need to crash here for?"

Her whole body tensed. I started to wonder if that was the wrong thing to ask, but then she slowly looked over at me. I could tell that asking me for help was killing her inside. And that was like a knife to my gut.

"A day? The weekend? I don't really have money, but I'm sure I can figure something out by then."

I stroked my chin as I studied her. I didn't like the idea of Claire being so close to me, invading my space. My feelings were confusing, and there was no way I'd be able to analyze them if she was there when I woke up and when I went to sleep. But I also didn't like the idea of her staying at a stranger's house.

So, despite my better judgement, I scrubbed my face with my hand and then focused my attention back on her. "If you stay, you work."

Her eyes widened. "What kind of work?"

"The bar. You can help me there."

She looked skeptical.

"Wash dishes. Wait tables. Break up fights."

Her eyebrows went up.

"Okay, maybe not break up fights, but anything that I need you to do."

She narrowed her eyes as she studied me.

I stepped back, grabbed the edge of the door, and started to shut it. "Or you can find another place to stay."

Her hands went up, and she stepped toward me. "Okay. Okay. I'll do whatever you need me to do."

I paused and let the silence between us grow heavy. Then I took a step back and waved her in. "You're in."

She didn't move. Instead, she stared at the inside of my house like it was her new cage. It felt like a gut punch, but I shook it off. Of course, she wasn't excited that she was going to spend time with her ex. She'd spent so many years running away from this place—from me—only to end up right back here.

Fate had a cruel sense of humor.

I took a few steps back before pushing my hands through my damp hair, no doubt causing it to stand on end. "Take your time. I'm going to get dressed."

Claire's reaction to coming inside had my body pricking with irritation. My house wasn't that bad. Sure, I lived like a bachelor, but I also helped take care of Gramps when he was in town. It needed to be tidy for him.

I shut my bedroom door and made my way over to my dresser, anger building up inside of me. She was the one who didn't show up that night all those years ago. She was the one who didn't talk to me for over a week. And when I finally nailed her down, she told me that she was done with me, our relationship, and...everything.

I had to watch from the sidelines as she dated other guys at school, graduated, and left this town so fast that her car left skid marks on the pavement.

She took my heart and pulverized it. So, for her to stand out there like my house was diseased was outright uncalled for.

I aggressively pulled my black t-shirt over my head before I pulled on my jeans and made my way into the bathroom to style my hair before brushing my teeth. Once I felt a bit more like myself, I grabbed my keys and wallet from my dresser and made my way into the kitchen. Aunt Pricilla's familiar voice caused me to stop in my tracks.

"I just don't know what that girl is doing back in Harmony and why she's here in Jax's backyard. Do you think..." She paused, and I could feel her judgement even though there was a wall between us. "Do you think Jax got back together with her?"

My grandfather's soft voice was too hard to hear this far away. But even though I couldn't hear what he was saying, I could tell by the cadence of his voice that he was trying to defend me.

Unable to stand here and listen to this anymore, I rounded the corner and stepped into the kitchen. "Hey, Aunt P," I said as I made my way over to the fridge. Gramps was sitting at the table with a coffee mug and a newspaper in front of him.

Aunt Pricilla was leaning over the sink, staring out the window. She startled and pulled back, her eyes wide. "Jaxson," she said, her hand going to her chest. "You almost gave me a heart attack."

I shot her a look before grabbing a bottle of orange juice and finding a glass in the cupboard next to the fridge. "What are you doing staring out at my backyard?"

Aunt Pricilla seemed to have composed herself. She was standing off to the side with her arms folded and her eyes narrowed. "Why is Claire Hodges out there with a dog?"

I eyed my aunt from over the cup of orange juice that I was downing. I held her gaze until I finished and then walked over to rinse out the cup and set it in the sink. My gaze drifted out the window, where I saw Claire playing tug-of-war with Carmel. She was smiling and laughing—an expression I hadn't seen in a long time. I hated how warm it made my body feel.

"She's staying here for a few days," I said nonchalantly.

Aunt Pricilla's eyebrows went up. "She's staying *here*?"

I didn't want to have this conversation. I didn't want to talk to my aunt about Claire. I wasn't even sure how I felt about any of it, and I didn't want to try to unpack it when Claire could come into the house at any moment.

"Don't you have places to be?" I asked as I turned to face her. I leaned against the counter and folded my arms.

Aunt Pricilla glanced down at her watch. "Yes. I have a

meeting with my designer today." She crossed the room, kissed my grandfather on the cheek, and grabbed her purse. "It was great spending the weekend with you, Dad," she said.

He was reading the paper, so he just waved her away before grabbing his mug of coffee and taking a sip.

Aunt Pricilla straightened and looked at me. I could tell she wanted to say something, and there wasn't anything I could do to stop it. "Jax," she started.

I groaned. "Aunt P, let's not do this."

She held up her hand. "A Robinson and a Hodges do not make a good pair. I thought you learned this. Missy will stop at nothing to see that this family pays for past mistakes, even if that means spreading lies about your parents all over town."

Movement in the backyard drew my attention. Claire patted Carmel on the head and then turned and started making her way toward the back door that led right into the kitchen.

Even though I agreed with her about Claire's mom, this was not the time or the place to have this conversation. "I'm done talking about this," I said as I stepped forward with my hands raised, as if that was all it would take to silence my aunt.

"I'm just saying you need to be careful. I know you have a history with her, but that doesn't mean you should jump back into anything. It's best to stay away from Claire and that entire family."

I should have known she was going to keep going. I made my way over to the door and stood in front of it, holding the handle so Claire couldn't turn it. "I got it, Aunt P," I said, shooting Gramps a desperate look.

"I think he understands you, Pricilla." Grandpa was staring at her from over his spectacles.

Aunt Pricilla opened and closed her mouth a few times as she glanced between Grandpa and me. Then she harrumphed and pulled her purse strap higher up onto her shoulder. "I can see that I'm no longer wanted."

I felt the door handle start to turn, so I gripped it hard. "Bye," I said, hoping she didn't realize that I was attempting to keep Claire at bay.

She studied me and then sighed before she nodded and turned to Grandpa. "I'll see you for dinner on Saturday?"

He had returned to reading the paper. "Yep," he said as he turned a page.

"Bye, Jax," she said.

I gave her a quick smile. I felt Claire attempt the handle again, but I held onto it tightly. Thankfully, Aunt Pricilla didn't linger, and a few seconds later, I heard the front door open and close. I jumped back from the door, turned the handle, and pulled it open.

An exasperated Claire met my gaze. Her cheeks were flushed.

"Were you holding the door handle so I couldn't get in?"

I swung the door a few times. "This door sticks some-times. I was trying to open it on my end."

Gramps snorted, and I shot him a look. If he noticed, he didn't acknowledge it.

I turned back to Claire, who was eyeing me. "Right," she said slowly.

I stepped out of the way and waved her in. "Come on in."

She stepped inside and glanced around. "I put Carmel in the backyard. I hope that's okay."

I shut the door behind her and nodded. "That's fine. She can sleep in the garage at night."

Claire wrapped her arms around her chest as she stood in the middle of the room. She glanced over at Gramps, who didn't look up from his paper, which I appreciated. When she glanced back over at me, I could tell she felt uncomfortable. I couldn't blame her.

After all, our families had been at war with each other for decades. It was hard to know who you could trust and who you couldn't.

"Come on, I'll show you where you can sleep," I said over my shoulder as I led her down the hallway to my spare bedroom.

Luckily, I didn't have to convince her to follow me this time. I could hear her footsteps behind me as I entered the room. The bed was old, but the sheets were clean. My squat rack and weights were on the other side of the room.

"Is this going to be okay?" Claire asked as she nodded toward my home gym.

"It'll be fine. I'll work out when you're not in here."

She nodded as she glanced around. "And it's only for a few days while I figure out where I'm going to stay."

I wanted to tell her that she could stay as long as she wanted to. I wanted to tell her that I was happy she was here. That maybe, we might get some closure on the time we spent together so many years ago.

But there was no way I was going to say any of that. Instead, I just nodded. "Sounds good."

She walked over to the bed and sat down. I wasn't sure if she wanted me in here or not, so I turned and made my way to the door. Just before I stepped out into the hallway, her voice stopped me in my tracks.

"Jax?"

I glanced over at her, hating and loving the sound of my name on her lips. "Yeah?"

"Thanks."

She looked so small and fragile, and all I wanted to do was protect her. But she wasn't mine to protect. This was just a temporary arrangement, that was all.

"Of course. But you're not staying here for free." I knocked on the doorframe. "Get settled. We are leaving in an hour. We've got work to do."

She nodded. I made my way down the hallway and back into the kitchen, where Gramps sat. He hadn't moved from his spot and was currently sipping his coffee. He stared at me over his mug. His bushy eyebrows were raised, and I could see the questions he had for me. But I didn't want to digest them right now.

"Not you, too," I said as I started gathering the ingredients for my normal morning protein shake.

"I didn't say anything."

I glanced over my shoulder at him. "Yeah, but you want to."

He shrugged, set his mug down, and returned to his newspaper. "Just be careful."

I set down the measuring cup I used to scoop protein powder into the blender. "I'll be fine."

He snorted but didn't say anything.

I glared at the milk I was pouring into the powder. I was going to be fine. I was. I was just irritated that my entire family thought I couldn't handle myself around Claire. They were the reason my agitation level was at an all-time high, not her. They were the reason my mind felt like it was racing and nothing I was doing seemed to calm it down.

I was going to be fine having Claire Hodges living in my house for the next few days.

I flipped on the blender and let the whirring sound of the motor mute the thoughts in my head. I grabbed the measuring cups and dumped them in the sink.

I was going to be...fine.

3

JUNIPER

SWEET TEA & SOUTHERN GENTLEMAN

I sat on my childhood bed with my wet hair wrapped up in a towel, listening to my mother in the kitchen. I could tell that she was attempting to talk in a hushed voice, but, as always, she was failing.

Betty Godwin was not a soft talker.

"I know, Betty, but she's been through a lot. It's best to just let her take her time."

A soft smile grew on my lips as I pulled at the towel and let my hair tumble down around me. I set it down next to me and began to comb my fingers through my damp hair. I could always depend on Dad to stand up for me. He and I were similar. We liked our autonomy. We were quiet and reserved, and it drove my mother nuts.

"She's been here for three days, Rich. It's time she talked. Haven't you seen those stories about people who keep their feelings pent up for too long and then they kill their parents?"

I glanced over toward the door. Did she seriously just say that? The heavy pause told me Dad's expression had to be similar to mine. A mixture of confusion and annoyance.

"I don't think that's Juniper."

Mom's exasperated sigh created an image of her throwing her hands up in the air. And when it was followed by clanging, I knew she'd made her way over to the oven, where she was starting to rage cook.

I shook my hair out and stood. I grabbed my towel and hung it on the hook behind the bathroom door. I needed to go save my dad before Mom decided he was no longer necessary and cooked him.

Just as I turned around, I caught my reflection in the mirror. My dark hair framed my face and accented my pale skin. But that wasn't what I was looking at. It was the brown and yellowish bruise that surrounded my eye.

The one that Kevin gave me.

A wave of nausea washed over me. I clutched my midsection and hurried over to the toilet and sat down. I hunched over my stomach and inhaled through my nose, releasing my breath slowly from my lips. I closed my eyes and focused my mind.

I was stronger than this. I'd left. I was never going back to him. We were over.

My hair fell around my face, caging me in. I glanced

down at the ground, forcing myself to believe that I was safe, even though I didn't feel that way.

Kevin was a Proctor. His family ruled this town. No matter where I went, he was going to find me. There was a part of me that was surprised he hadn't come banging down the door the day after I arrived here. But the other part of me knew that, to Kevin, image was everything.

He wasn't one to make mistakes. Everything he did was calculated. If he wanted me back, he'd find a way to do it that made him look clean, and me dirty.

I squeezed my eyes shut and focused back on my breathing.

I was tired of letting him have this much power over me. I was not going back to him, even if he wanted me to. I'd left, and I was going to be strong no matter what.

Luckily, the Tilt-A-Whirl feeling in my stomach had subsided, and I no longer felt like I was going to vomit. I straightened, took a few deep breaths, and stood. I faced the mirror once more, grabbed my concealer, and did my best to cover up the remnants of his handiwork on my face.

I pulled my hair up into a ponytail, straightened my clothes, and turned off the light. I headed over to my door and out into the hallway. Mom and Dad were quiet now. I could hear movement in the kitchen, which told me Mom was cooking, but other than that, I didn't know where people were.

I rounded the corner and two separate gazes landed on me. Dad was sitting at the table, scrolling on his phone, and

Mom was just where I'd pictured her, standing in front of the stove with steam rising from the pan in front of her.

"Morning, sweetheart," Dad said before he shot Mom a warning look.

She narrowed her eyes at him but didn't say anything as she turned back to the food she was cooking.

"Hey," I said. I walked over to the mug tree and grabbed a mug. I set it down in front of the coffee maker and poured myself some coffee. "Smells good, Ma."

Mom's shoulders tensed, but she quickly relaxed them as she glanced over at me. "I'm making scrambled eggs. Do you want some?"

My stomach growled. It seemed to have forgotten the nausea from a few minutes ago. "Yes, please," I said as I headed over to the table, where Dad was pulling out a nearby chair.

"Did you sleep well?" he asked.

I nodded. I picked up my mug and held it between my hands. I inhaled the French vanilla scent and closed my eyes.

"I'm glad to hear it."

I glanced over at him and smiled.

Silence filled the kitchen. Any other time, I would have enjoyed sitting with my parents, where the only sound was my mom cooking. But today, the air was filled with unasked questions all directed at me.

They wanted answers that I wasn't ready to give them.

"I was hoping that I could come help at the store today,"

I said, unable to take the tension in the room any longer.

They both looked at me. Mom's eyebrows were raised, and she was holding a spatula in her hand. "Really?"

I nodded. "It would be good to get out of the house. Talk to people. I mean, if I'm back, I might as well get acclimated." I forced a smile, hoping they would buy the lie I was selling them.

I watched as Mom and Dad attempted to stealthily exchange a concerned glance. I sighed and leaned back in my chair. "I'm not fragile. I won't break. I can handle scanning food at the store."

"It's not that we don't think you can do it..." Dad started but never really finished his thought.

"We're just worried that you might run into a Proctor or someone might ask you where Kevin is..." Mom also let her voice trail off. They both had questions that neither was asking.

"I doubt the Proctors will come into the store. They go to the Whole Foods in Pearl County. And Kevin is in Texas. He's not here." Running after his wife wasn't really his thing. At least, not until he had a plan.

Mom studied me before she glanced over at Dad. "What do you think, honey?" she asked as she turned back to the pan and clicked off the burner. Then she lifted the pan off the stove and started to dish up the eggs onto plates she'd set out.

Dad cleared his throat, drawing my attention over to him. He was mentally chewing on his decision.

"I'll be fine," I said.

He glanced over at me and then nodded. "You're a grown woman. If you think you're ready, I'm not going to stop you." His gaze drifted to my eye like it had done every day since I'd come home, and a moment later, his right hand clenched.

Not wanting to address it, I just forced a smile. "I'll be fine."

Thankfully, Mom delivered the plates to the table, and we ate in silence. The rollercoaster my stomach had been on seemed to settle with each bite, which helped me clear my head and focus my thoughts.

I'd camped out in my room the last few days, and I was excited to get out. It'd been a while since my last visit to Harmony. I came back here with Kevin last year, but that was just for the weekend. And it was just to see his father get some award for donating money so the medical center could get a new emergency room.

On that trip, we didn't have time to walk around the town. I'd been allowed to invite my parents to a dinner, but that was all the time Kevin gave me for them. Back then, I would have done anything for that man. I thought that he loved me and wanted what was best for me.

I'd thought wrong.

The sound of forks scraping on porcelain marked the end of breakfast. I stood before either of my parents, so I started to gather their plates to take them to the sink.

"I'll wash up," I said over my shoulder as I turned the

water on. Mom gathered the rest of the dirty dishes, and Dad wiped off the table.

Once they were done, they left me alone to wash up while they got ready to leave for the store. I was drying my hands when they walked back into the kitchen fifteen minutes later, Mom with her purse slung over her shoulder and Dad carrying his shoes. I hurried to get ready, and we walked out the front door together.

I rode with them to Godwin's. Dad parked behind the store in his familiar spot. I pulled open the back door—making sure to stop the door before it hit the tree stump that had been there since I was a teenager—and climbed out.

I followed behind them as we made our way to the back door next to the loading dock. Dad pulled his keys from his pocket and unlocked it. Mom was already pulling out her readers as she headed into the back office and turned the light on. I lingered in the doorway while she turned on her monitor.

She glanced at me from above her readers. "I've got some orders to sort out. How about you go wipe down the registers before we open?"

I glanced toward the front of the store and nodded. "I can do that."

She settled down in her chair. "Perfect."

Dad had disappeared between the rows of stock, so I made my way through the swinging doors into the store. The sun was just beginning to come up, casting its faint morning glow through the windows and spilling around me.

The exit signs were the brightest light in the store, illuminating the air above each door. I let the door swing closed behind me as I made my way to the registers.

I lost myself in cleaning the belt, the register keys, and the counter. I was on the last checkout when suddenly, all the lights in the store came on. I blinked a few times as my eyes adjusted.

A knock on the sliding doors in the front drew my attention over. Katie and Sal were standing there, each holding a thermos of what I could only assume was coffee. I could see the steam rising from the little opening where they would take a sip.

I gave them a small wave as I rounded the register and made my way over to them.

"I've got the key," Dad said from behind me.

I turned just in time to see him walk past with his keys jingling. He grabbed the set, riffled through them until he found the right one, and then unlocked the door and pushed it open.

Katie and Sal murmured good morning and then headed to their respective places. Katie in the bakery and Sal behind the meat counter.

"Registers cleaned?" Dad asked as he pushed the doors shut and locked them. He turned to look at me for a moment before glancing toward the registers.

"I just finished the last one."

He nodded. "Mom and I were talking and think it

would be good to have you stocking some shelves this morning. Think you can do that?"

I chewed my lip. I knew it was ridiculous to think that Mrs. Proctor and her flock of followers would ever come into my family's grocery store—they were *import food from fancy places* kind of people. But if I was wrong and she showed up to find me stocking shelves, I'm not sure I would survive.

And if Kevin got wind of where I was...

My heart started to pound. I closed my eyes for a second and shook my head. I needed to stop thinking like that. I'd told Kevin we were done. I'd walked away. There was no reason for him to follow me here. He was cheating on me. I'm sure he felt relief when I left.

Now he could date and sleep with whomever he wanted to.

I didn't want to break down in front of Dad, and I wasn't ready for Mom to hear what really happened, so I swallowed against all the emotions that had lodged themselves in my throat and nodded. "I can do that," I whispered. My throat was hoarse, so I coughed a few times, hoping Dad didn't notice.

He was eyeing me when I brought my gaze back to him, but thankfully he didn't say anything. Instead, he just nodded as he hooked his keys back onto his belt loop and moved to walk past me.

"I'm finishing up logging some inventory in the back, and then I'll be out with the cash to fill the registers. Mom is going to take the morning shift, and then Jordan will be in later to take over." He paused and glanced down at me. "Do you think you could hop on a register if we get busy?"

"Yeah, I can do that."

He nodded and then disappeared. The sound of the swinging doors marked his departure. I sighed and leaned my hip against the nearby register. I closed my eyes and allowed my body to relax. Thoughts of Kevin were going to bother me, that was just a fact.

He was the man I thought I was going to spend the rest of my life with. He was the man that I married. The man I was going to start a family with. Even though he broke me down when I was with him, there was a part of me that couldn't see my future without him. I'd always believed he could change. He hurt me when he got angry, so I strived to always make him happy.

My stomach began to churn, and there was no way I wanted another repeat of this morning. I pressed on it a few times, hoping to dispel the butterflies that seemed to be locked in there, but nothing I did could get them out.

Spit began to form in my mouth, so I swallowed it down and took a few deep breaths. I tipped my face toward the ceiling, which seemed to help lessen the nausea.

Every day, these feelings would fade. Every day that I was away from Kevin, I was going to feel better. I had to believe that was true.

If not, I was going to break. And if I broke, I wasn't going to be able to put myself back together. No matter how hard I tried.

4

CLAIRE

SWEET TEA &
SOUTHERN GENTLEMAN

"I think I can just drive myself," I said as I eyed Jax's truck. I was standing a few feet away from where Jax stood next to the open driver's door. He wore sunglasses, so I couldn't quite see his expression, but I felt like I was melting. It didn't help that the sun was peeking over the top of the trees. Its warm rays caused my skin to prick with sweat.

"Are you serious?" Jax asked. He stepped around the open door so he could face me fully. He crossed his arms, and even though I couldn't see his eyes, I could feel his stare.

I held onto the strap of my purse like it was a lifeline. Like it would somehow give me the strength to defy this man. I was confused why he wanted me to get into his truck. I was an independent woman. I could drive myself.

"I just think that I should drive myself," I managed, trying to sound more confident than I felt.

Jax paused but then sighed. "Fine. Do what you want."

He made his way back around the driver's door and climbed inside.

The sound of his door shutting caused me to jump. I didn't wait for him to change his mind. I pulled out my keys as I hurried over to my car. Once inside, I slipped the keys into the ignition and turned.

The sound of the ignition slipping filled the air followed by a god-awful scraping. I stopped trying to start the car and sat back. I must have done something wrong. I pulled the key out and then stuck it back in the ignition.

I hesitated before I turned the key only to be met with the same sound. I cursed under my breath as I leaned forward and rested my forehead on the steering wheel. Why was this happening to me?

I tried to start my car one more time, but when nothing happened, I tossed the keys in the passenger seat.

The sound of knocking on the window next to me caused me to yelp and snap my head toward the noise. Red-hot heat radiated from my neck. I moaned as I brought my hand to the pain and held my neck, like that would stop it. I closed my eyes for a moment, waiting for the pain to subside before I reached down and grabbed the door handle.

"Are you ready to stop being so stubborn and get in my truck with me?" Jax asked. He was holding open the door with one hand while the other was resting on the roof of my car.

I could smell his cologne, and his gaze made my whole body react as he stared down at me. I hated that my heart picked up speed when he was around. I hated the memory that flooded my mind of him caging me in and pressing me against my family's basement room wall before kissing me until I couldn't breathe. I hated that I remembered what it felt like for him to touch me...to kiss me.

Why couldn't I have amnesia for that part of my life?

"Claire?"

I startled and winced as pain shot up my neck once more. I groaned and cradled my neck as I glared over at him. "What?"

He took a step back. "Nothing. You just went glassy-eyed on me. I wanted to make sure that you were okay." He leaned down so he was at eye level. "You okay?"

I grabbed my keys and purse and turned to face him, ignoring how his proximity made my heart pound. "I'm fine," I said as I started to climb out of my car.

Like two magnets, the closer I got to him, the more he pulled back. By the time I stepped out, Jax had moved to stand a few feet off. I walked around the door and then slammed it closed.

I pulled my purse strap back up onto my shoulder as I headed toward his car. My neck muscles ached, but I wasn't going to let him know that I was injured. I was going to be the strong and independent woman I'd forced myself to be when I left this town.

The last thing I needed him to know was that I was floundering and his mere presence caused my entire body to feel as if it were trapped on a Tilt-A-Whirl.

I grabbed the passenger door handle and pulled, but the door didn't budge, causing my entire hand to jerk back. I growled as I glanced up at Jax. He was sitting on the driver's seat and sheepishly raised his hand as the sound of the doors unlocking filled the air around me. I yanked on the handle and climbed onto the seat.

"Sorry about that," he said, his voice softer than it had been earlier.

"It's fine," I said as I shut the door and then felt for my seatbelt, wincing when I tried to turn my head. "I'll have to call a tow truck to take my car to the shop."

I could feel Jax's gaze on me before he put his car into reverse and backed out of his driveway. "You know I work on cars, right?"

I sighed as I kept my gaze out the window. "I know that."

A silence fell between us. I could tell that he wanted to say more but didn't know how, and I was certain that I didn't want to hear what he had to say. I needed to shut down any deep emotional conversations he might want to have. Staying with him was temporary. He knew that. And I certainly needed to remind myself of that if I was going to have any chance of surviving.

"It's best for us to keep our distance," I whispered as I kept my focus on the trees out my window.

"Huh?"

I turned and instantly pulled back when I saw Jax had leaned closer to me. He had his wrist resting on the steering wheel with his other elbow resting on the console between us. He looked so...relaxed. It made my heart hurt.

His gaze suddenly met mine. I quickly diverted my gaze out the windshield. My cheeks warmed, and I feared he could see my blush. I reached up and rubbed my cheek, wincing as the movement caused my neck to move.

But he couldn't know the kind of reaction I was having to him. I needed to keep my head on straight and focus on getting a place to stay while Rose was in recovery.

"You said something?" His familiar voice washed over me like my favorite song.

I frowned, forcing my body to stop reacting this way to him. "I think it's best for us to keep our distance," I said again, louder.

From the corner of my eye, I could see him study me before he turned his attention back to the road. The silence between us was deafening as I waited for him to respond. He slowed the truck to a stop in front of a red light. He closed his eyes and pinched the bridge of his nose before opening them again and glancing over at me. "It's just a car, Claire. I can help you fix your car."

I hated that everything about him was so familiar. I hated that he was there for me when my mother threw me out. I hated that he wasn't yelling at me or telling me to leave him alone.

I hated that it didn't seem like he hated me at all.

I held his gaze, and we just sat there, looking at each other. I wanted him to know that I was sorry for the night I didn't show up. Mom had convinced me that his mother and my father were having an affair. I left town thinking that our relationship had been a ruse. An effort on his part to destroy our family. I realized too late that it might not have been true, but us breaking up was for the best. My mom was toxic, and she would stop at nothing to keep me from having a relationship with a Robinson.

Jax needed to stay away from me. Even though I'd asked to stay at his house, I was determined to make this a short stay. My heart couldn't handle anything longer. I only had so much strength.

A Hodges and a Robinson were like oil and water. A happily ever after was never in the cards for us. And he knew that. I knew he knew that.

"I don't want you to touch it," I whispered, fighting the tears that were forming. "I don't...trust you." The last two words were barely audible, but his eyes widened, and he pulled back. He'd heard.

And the meaning wasn't lost on him.

He turned his attention back to the red light, his muscles rippling as he set his jaw. He gripped the steering wheel and stared straight ahead, like the traffic light held the answer to all of life's problems.

I wanted to take it back. I wanted to say something to ease the tension in the car, but I knew it was futile. He hated me now. Good. That's what I needed.

I held my purse in my lap as he drove the rest of the way to the pub. He didn't bother to talk or turn on the radio, so we just rode in silence. His wheels kicked up gravel as he pulled behind the pub and took a sharp left into one of the only parking spots back there.

As soon as his engine was off and his key was out of the ignition, he grabbed a pile of papers from the back—his chest brushing my shoulder for only a second—before he yanked open the driver's door and climbed out.

He didn't wait for me to follow. He slammed the door and crossed the parking lot to the back door in long strides. I let out the breath I'd been holding as soon as he disappeared through the door. My shoulders slumped as I closed my eyes, hating myself for what I'd said to him.

The truth was, I trusted Jax. More than he could ever know. I wanted him back in my life. Seeing him was torture. But no matter how much we bent our realities to create a relationship, we were never meant to be together.

I brushed my fingertips under my eyes to gather any tears that wanted to fall. The last thing I needed was to go into the pub with smudged eye makeup that would let everyone know I'd been upset.

I needed to be strong, and I needed to have focus.

The back door opened slightly, and I saw Remus, Jax's best friend from high school, poke his head around the edge of the door. His gaze landed on me, and he held it for a moment before he disappeared back into the pub, shutting the door behind him.

I took in a deep breath. This was going to be interesting.

I knew Remus didn't like me after I called things off

with Jax. He'd made it pretty clear on multiple occasions that I was no longer wanted in their group of friends. So having to spend the next few days working alongside him was going to be...interesting.

I was not looking forward to it.

I pulled my phone from my purse and swiped it on. I was going to check on Rose to see how things were going, and then I'd go in and face whatever was going on in the pub. I was sure Remus was going to have a lot of questions for Jax.

I located the hospital's number and held my breath as I waited for someone to pick up.

"Harmony Medical Center; this is Diane. How can I help you?"

I proceeded to explain who I was and who I was asking after. Diane told me that Rose was out of surgery and was recovering. Tears pricked my eyes once more as I thanked her for letting me know.

She told me that Rose was resting but should be able to see patients later in the evening. I wasn't sure when I was going to get done at the pub, so I told her that I would plan on coming by tomorrow morning, and I asked her if she would pass that information along. She said she'd let Rose's nurse know.

We said goodbye, and I hung up and slipped my phone back into my purse. I closed my eyes and tipped my head back, resting it on the headrest behind me. I took in a few deep breaths as a smile crept across my face.

Rose was going to be okay. The stint surgery went well, and she was on the mend. I'd never in my life felt more scared than when I saw Rose on the ground like that. It was how I was supposed to feel about my mother when she'd needed surgery...but I hadn't. Rose was my mother in more ways than one.

I couldn't lose her.

I needed a moment to compose myself, so I pulled down the visor and checked my makeup. Even though I had two almost-cries today, my mascara and eyeliner looked on point. I took in a deep breath and forced my face to look determined and focused. Then I flipped the visor back up and pulled the door handle.

I slipped my purse strap up onto my shoulder as I made my way across the gravel drive. It crunched under my feet. Butterflies assaulted my stomach as I neared the door.

I wasn't sure what I was going to find on the other side. I knew there were two people in that building who didn't like me. I could just turn around, call a ride share, and leave this place.

I shook my head as I slowly let out my breath. Very few places were going to allow Carmel, especially now that she was further along in her pregnancy.

Jax had a moral obligation to help with her, so it was in my best interest to stay there. Jax wouldn't make me leave.

I grasped the handle to the back door, the cool metal shocking my skin. I steeled my nerves before I turned the handle and pulled.

5

JAX

SWEET TEA & SOUTHERN GENTLEMAN

I cursed under my breath as the back door to the pub slammed behind me. The walls of this forty-year-old structure shuddered from the impact, but I didn't care.

Claire didn't trust me? *Me?*

I wasn't the one who left. I wasn't the one who walked away. I was going to propose to her the night she ripped my heart from my chest and stomped on it. My hand instantly went to the necklace I wore around my neck. Hanging from it was a small silver ring with a sapphire affixed to it.

I hated that I still wore it, but I couldn't seem to let it go. So, it stayed, hung around my neck like a weight, reminding me of everything I'd lost.

"Hey, boss," Remus' voice caused me to jump. I instantly dropped my hand as he rounded the corner, folded his arms, and leaned against the doorframe. He frowned as he studied me. "Why do you look like you just committed a crime?"

I scrubbed my face and rolled my shoulders. "I'm fine," I said as I moved to walk past him. Since he was crowding the door, I had to turn to the side to slip through. I made my way down the hall to my office and flipped the light on. The fluorescent bulbs blinked a few times before they fully illuminated the room.

I dropped the invoices I'd been carrying onto my desk and shook my mouse to turn the monitor on. Remus was now occupying my office door with his arms crossed and the same skeptical expression on his face. I pretended not to notice, hoping he'd give up, but he didn't.

I sighed and turned to face him. "What?" I asked, allowing the annoyance I felt to seep through the air. If he was going to poke the bear, he needed to know I wasn't going to play nice.

"Why do you look like..." His voice drifted off at the same time his eyes narrowed. "The only reason you've looked like this in the past was when..." Light shown in his gaze now. He knew. And I hated that he'd figured it out. "I heard she was back in town."

"Claire just needed a place to stay while Rose is in the hospital," I hurriedly blurted out.

His eyebrows went up and a mischievous looked passed over his eyes. "She's staying with you?"

Dammit.

"Listen, she needed a place to stay. I told her she could

stay with me." It made sense in my head. But Remus clearly
didn't see it that way.

"So...she's your guest?"

I scowled at him. I hated that he was prodding me like
this. "She's not my guest."

"She's a tenant. She's paying rent?"

I frowned. "Don't you have some booze to stock?"

"So, she's not paying you."

I collapsed into my desk chair and scrubbed my face
before tipping my head back and staring up at the ceiling. "I
told her she needed to work at the pub to pay me back."

Remus was quiet, and for a moment I allowed myself to
wonder if he'd actually decided to go find some work to do. I
peeked over at him to see that he was still standing in my
office door staring at me.

His gaze returned to mine, and I could see all the questions he had but he couldn't quite figure out which one to
ask. "When does she come in?"

Tired of this conversation, I shook my mouse, and the
screen slowly turned on. I clicked on my emails and opened
the first unread one. "She's already here," I said as I started
to skim a spam email. I clicked on the trash and opened the
next one.

"She's here?" He pointed his finger at the floor. "Like,
now?"

I nodded. "She's in my truck if you want to go see." I was
desperate to get him out of my office so I could have a
moment of silence to think.

Remus hooted as he clapped his hands. "Hell yeah, I want to go see."

Regret rushed through my body, but by the time I moved to stop him, he was long gone. I collapsed in my chair and rested my elbows on the armrests. I used my toes to push my chair from side to side as I stared at my steepled fingers.

Remus was the third person this morning who told me that allowing Claire Hodges back into my life was a bad idea. He was also the third person I'd chosen to outright ignore. They didn't know my mind. They didn't know my heart.

After Claire left, I built a fortress around my heart so high that no woman could ever penetrate it—much less the woman who caused the construction of said wall in the first place. I was done with Claire. Sure, I made stupid mistakes like suggesting I fix her car. But she did right by me when she told me that I could jump in a lake. Her saying she didn't trust me and that she was going to figure her car out on her own was exactly what I needed to hear.

I just needed to be smacked down once, and I would never make that mistake again. I scoffed as I pushed against the armrest so I could sit up. I was over Claire.

"Over," I mouthed to the emails on my monitor.

I did everything in my power to force Claire from my mind as I lost myself in deleting spam emails and paying invoices from my alcohol vendors. Things felt normal...until I realized that Remus still hadn't come back.

I stared out to the hallway as if I could suddenly acquire the power to see through walls. Where was he?

Was he talking to Claire?

Panic filled my chest as I turned off my monitor and stood. I haphazardly pushed my chair back under my desk as I made my way out into the hallway. I didn't hear voices, but that worried me more.

Did he have her cornered outside? Was he trapping her in my truck?

My hands instantly fisted at that thought as I walked toward the back door. I should have never told him that she was here. I should have never trusted him with that information. I knew he would never hurt her. But he'd been clear since we were teens; he didn't like Claire, but he tolerated her because she had been my girlfriend. After we broke up, he didn't hold back the dislike he had for her family.

I was an idiot.

Just as I rounded the last corner to the dead-end hallway where the back door was, a figure ran straight into my chest. I was so startled that my arms instantly surrounded them and pulled them to my chest so they wouldn't take a nose-dive toward the floor. I staggered to keep myself from falling.

The *eep* that emerged from them was soft and feminine, and it was in that moment I realized who I was hugging.

Claire.

Her hair smelled like peaches and cream. Her body fit so perfectly against mine. I could feel her curves and I knew her figure. It felt like coming home. She was everything that

I remembered, and yet, there were parts of her that were new.

She was different. I was different. And yet, our memories seemed to fill the gap between us so perfectly.

"Jax," she finally said as she shook her head a bit as if she were trying to get her hair out of her face. She tipped her head back and looked up at me. "Let go of me."

Out of instinct, I looked down and then inwardly cursed myself. Why did I do that? Her lips were dangerously close to mine. They were shiny and red. And for a split second, I wonder if they felt the same. Or were they different, too?

I hated that I wanted to know. The memory of having her this close to me was going to haunt me late at night when I couldn't fall asleep.

This was my own personal hell.

"Well, if it isn't *Claire Bear*." Remus' voice sounded from behind me.

I instantly dropped my arms and took a big step back. Remus stepped up next to me in the hallway with his arms crossed. He shot me a quizzical but knowing look before he turned his attention to Claire, who was busy sorting her hair out.

"Hey, Remus," she said, not bothering to look up at him.

"Jax told me you were back. Although I was surprised that you felt like my best friend"— he clapped me on the back— "and this old establishment were good enough for you."

"Remus," I hissed under my breath.

Claire's cheeks had turned pink, and her eyes were inky black as she drew her gaze upwards to focus on Remus. I could tell that she was embarrassed, but she was also mad. And I didn't like that my friend was causing her to feel this way.

"No, no. I think she should know what she did when she didn't show up that night. When she broke up with you the next day." He wrapped his arm around my shoulders and pulled me next to him. "This man is my brother, and you hurt him."

This was not what I wanted. I didn't want Claire to know what she did to me. I wanted her to believe that the moment she walked away from me, I forgot her. It was the only way I was going to survive her being here.

"Was that the delivery truck?" I snaked my arm up around Remus' neck before pulling him down into a head-lock. "I think that was the delivery truck. Let's go see," I said as I started to drag him down the hallway toward the back door.

"Jax!" he complained as he started to push on me to let him go.

But there was no way I was going to. Not when he seemed determined to run his mouth in front of Claire.

She sandwiched herself against the wall, so Remus and I could pass by her. I gave her a quick smile and then pushed open the door with my free hand and pulled my best friend out into the parking lot. I made sure the door was shut behind us before I let Remus go.

"What the hell, man?" he asked as he pulled away from me and straightened his shirt. His hand then went to his head to make sure that his hair was intact.

"You were speaking out your butt, Remus," I said as I started to pace in front of him. I pressed my hand onto the back of my neck and stretched with the hope that the tension building in my back would lessen.

"I was not."

I faced my friend. "Yes, you were."

He glowered at me. "I'm just standing up for you."

I sighed and tipped my face toward the sky before returning my gaze to him. "I understand that, but I don't need you to protect me. Just, let me handle Claire." I raised my hands as if I were waving the white flag of surrender. "Please."

He eyed me. I could see that he didn't want to say yes, but we'd been friends for so long. How could he say no to me?

"I need this. Checkmate?"

His expression softened at our code word. One we used when we needed the other person to trust us. We were nerds in middle school and competed on the chess team together. Back then he was struggling with how to explain what was happening with his abusive stepdad and alcoholic mom. All he had to say was *checkmate,* and I knew things were bad.

I hoped he'd understand in this situation.

"Checkmate?" he asked as he scrubbed his hand down

his face and then glanced back over at me.

"Checkmate."

I could see that he didn't want to give in, but I was grateful when he let out a growl and nodded his head. I walked over to him and clapped him on the shoulder. "It'll be fine. *I* will be fine." I gave him an encouraging smile.

He studied me. "I'll play nice, but the moment she acts shady, all bets are off."

I squeezed his shoulder. "I don't think she'll be here long enough to do anything." My heart clenched. I knew my heart had other desires, but I wasn't going to acknowledge them. Instead, I kept them in the lockbox in the darkest part of my mind.

Remus narrowed his eyes. "I hope not."

I sighed and gave Remus a weak smile. I loved my friend, I did, but he tended to shoot first and ask questions later. I knew it had a lot to do with his parents, but sometimes I needed him to be less intense.

But that was like asking water to be a bit less wet.

"I'm going inside," I said as I dropped my hand and made my way to the back door. "You coming?"

Remus stood rooted to the spot. "I need a minute."

"Sure." I tossed him a smile before I pulled the door open and made my way into the pub.

Claire wasn't in the hallway where I'd left her. Curious as to where she'd gone, I started looking for her. She wasn't in the storage room or my office, so I pushed through the swinging doors and into the bar. I scanned the room and almost gave up when her dark figure caught my eye.

She was standing on the dance floor, right in front of the stage. She had her arms wrapped around her body and her head tilted to the side. If I hadn't been staring as hard as I was, I wouldn't have noticed that she was slightly swaying from side to side. Like she was deep into a memory.

I almost didn't want to interrupt her, but I also couldn't leave her out here. I didn't open until three, but people still tried to day drink. I had to shoo two or three Harmony residents away from my front door on the regular. The last thing I needed was someone thinking I was letting people in early.

"Claire?" I whispered as I stepped closer to her.

She startled and glanced over at me. Her skin reddened as she dropped her hands before pressing them against her cheeks. "Sorry. I got lost in thought."

I raised my hands. "It's okay. I get it." I rested my hand on the dark oak bar. "Lots of memories here."

Her gaze drifted to my hand before she nodded. "Remus okay?"

I swallowed before I scoffed. "Remus? He's fine." She gave me a skeptical look. "He'll be fine."

"He hates me."

I shrugged. "Remus hates everyone."

"Not you." Her gaze was soft as she studied me.

"Not me," I repeated.

Her gaze hadn't left my face, and my heart was pounding. I could tell that she was curious, and I wanted her to ask the questions that I could see racing through her mind. But at the same time, I feared what they might expose.

"Remus is also crazy," I blurted out. I stuck out my thumb and pinkie finger and made the motion like I was drinking. "He day drinks."

She raised her eyebrows. "Really?"

I nodded my head, but then I slowed and changed it to a shake. "No, that was a lie. He doesn't day drink, and he's not crazy." I shoved my hands into my front pockets, fearing what I would do with them if they were free.

Claire closed her lips and drew her eyebrows together.

Maybe I should tell her that I day drink. I was sticking my foot so far into my mouth, that it had disappeared. Or the better option would be to just leave. Walk away and pretend that this conversation never happened. Would she forget it?

From the look on her face, it had been burned into her brain.

"I've got some orders to finish back in my office before the delivery gets here," I said as I started to turn and nodded toward the doors that led to the back.

"Okay," she said softly. She shrugged. "Anything you want me to do out here? After all, I'm on the clock." She gave me a quick smile. "I gotta earn my room and board."

I glanced around. The space behind the bar was a mess. "How about cleaning up back here?" I asked as I waved toward the space where Remus and I stood every night.

She rose up onto her tiptoes and glanced behind the bar. "Yeah, I can do that. Cleaning supplies are?"

I pointed toward the bathrooms in the back corner. "Bathroom closet."

She swung her hands in front of her and clapped them together. Then she rolled her shoulders. "Perfect. I'll get started."

I stood there, watching her. It still amazed me that she was here, standing in my pub. Sure, I'd dreamed that this day might come, but that was all it was. A dream. Not my reality.

But she was really here, and I was having a hard time digesting it.

"Great," I said, realizing that I was staring. I needed to get out of here. Now. "Well, I'm gonna go." I jutted my thumb toward the door.

Memories of people banging on the door before opening raced into my mind, so I turned back. "Just, stay out of sight. People are always trying to come in before we're open, and if they see you..." I shrugged.

She glanced to the left, toward the glass front door. "Yeah, I'll try."

"Great." I gave her a small smile and turned back around. I started toward the swinging doors but stopped when I heard Claire's voice.

"Jax?"

My jaw tightened, and I closed my eyes. I was never going to get used to the sound of my name on her lips. I fisted my hand, hating that she still had this much control over me. "Yeah?" I asked, tipping my head to the side, but I didn't turn around.

When she didn't answer right away, I contemplated turning around, but forced myself to stay still.

"Thanks." Her voice was soft, barely a whisper, but it sent shivers across my skin. Memories washed over me. Cuddling with her on my parents' couch after they went to bed, kissing her, talking to her in hushed tones. They made my entire body ache.

Ache for her. Ache for what we had.

"Of course," I said before I pushed through the swinging doors and entered the hallway. Once they shut behind me, I leaned against the wall, tipping my head up and cursing the feelings that were coursing through my body with every pump of my heart.

I wanted her back. And I was a fool to think I could handle letting her back into my life.

Remus was right. I was an idiot. But I couldn't turn her away. I could just pray I had the strength to keep my distance. Or my heart was going to break.

Again.

6

JUNIPER

SWEET TEA &
SOUTHERN GENTLEMAN

I don't know why, but the sight of whole pickled onions always made my stomach churn. Even when I was a child, I could never understand why people would eat those things. They looked like eyeballs without the irises.

I shuddered as I slid another jar onto the floor shelf. Maybe if I just didn't look at them, I would be okay.

Once the row was stocked, I moved on to stock pickles. Minus having to look at the onions, stocking shelves was soothing. I thrived in monotony. I could just let my mind relax as I slid items into their designated spots.

This was just what I needed.

"Juniper," Mom's voice was high-pitched and panicked. I turned to see her speed walk down the aisle toward me.

"Mom?" I asked as I stepped off my stool and faced her. "What's up?"

"I need you to take over on the register," she said when

she finally got to me. Her face was bright pink, and her eyes were darting all around.

"Okay," I said with a nod. Then I reached out and touched her arm. "Is everything okay?"

She shook her head. "Mrs. Valasquez fell, and I need to go to Harmony Medical Center since I'm her emergency contact."

"Of course. Go. I'll take care of the register."

She gave me a quick hug. "Thank you, sweetie. Dad already put you into the system. Your login code is your birth date." She pulled back and gave me a smile. "You can do this. I believe in you."

My eyebrows drew together. I wanted to ask her what that meant, but she was down the aisle before I could inquire. I decided to shake it off as I loaded the empty boxes onto the stock cart and pushed it through the back doors and into the stockroom. I quickly washed my hands and headed back out onto the floor.

There were only a few people in the store, and they were perusing the produce, so I took my time heading to the register. I filled my water bottle from the drinking fountain near the front. I headed down the register lane, grabbing a magazine as I went. When I got to the register, I punched in my code, and thankfully, running the checkout was just like riding a bike. You never forget.

I sat on the stool my mother normally leaned against as she rang up items. After a long sip of water, I grabbed the magazine and started flipping through it. My mother couldn't give me any side-eye since she was out of the store. She didn't like anyone doing anything but standing there looking ready for the next customer—even though I knew she hid a sudoku puzzle book in the zippered pouch she always brought up with her.

Fifteen minutes later, I was deep in a "where are they now?" article about celebrities from the nineties when I heard someone softly clear their throat next to me. My entire face heated as I closed the magazine and dumped it onto the shelf in front of me.

A woman who looked around my age with soft brown hair and a wide smile greeted me. She was holding a basket full of food.

"I am so sorry," I said as she put the basket on the conveyor belt.

"It's fine." She must have seen my embarrassment because she leaned forward. "Freddie Prinze Jr. was a surprise for me."

"Right?" I said as I started pulling her groceries out. "It's so crazy to me how someone can go from celebrity status to disappearing."

She chuckled and nodded. "It's crazy. And hard to understand when you live in a small town where everyone knows everyone."

"Definitely."

Silence built up around us. I could tell that she was trying to figure out who I was, so I decided to help her out.

"I'm Juniper," I said as I pointed to my name tag.

Her gaze followed my gesture before coming back to my face. "Abigail."

I reached across the register and shook her hand. "I'm Rich and Betty's daughter."

"Ah, yes. I've heard them talk about you."

"All good things, I hope."

She just smiled. "Your mom definitely missed you while you were gone."

My heart swelled at the thought. My parents might have disagreed with my choice in Kevin, but they always loved me. Even if I had pushed them away for so long.

"Thanks," I whispered, not wanting to get emotional in front of a stranger. "I've missed her, too."

I grabbed Abigail's avocados and set them on the scale. Then I began to flip through the produce booklet next to me.

"So, are you visiting or here to stay?"

I paused at Abigail's question. It was so loaded, and I didn't know how to answer it. She must have sensed my hesitation because she raised her hands. "I totally don't mean to pry. I know what it's like to just want to be left alone."

I shook my head as I repeated the avocado number in my head a few times, turned, and punched it into the register. "No, that's totally fine. I'm just...in a transition of sorts."

The avocado weight registered, and I pulled them off the scale and slipped them into a plastic bag next to me.

"I know what that feels like. My whole life has been a

transition of sorts, until..." A soft smile spread across her lips, and it intrigued me.

I paused and studied her. "A guy?"

Her cheeks flushed. "Is it obvious?"

"A little."

"His name is Sebastian—Bash. He works in New York, so I don't see him a lot. But he's coming in tonight." She waved to the food in the basket and in the plastic bags next to me. "Hence the food."

"Aww," I said. I was happy for her, but there was a part of me that hurt. I'd felt like that for a guy once. Kevin was the center of my world. Now, I didn't know what I was going to do. Going back to Kevin didn't seem like an option, but at the same time, I worried that he was the best I could do.

"How about you? Do you have someone in your life?"

I gave her a soft smile, but then my gaze drifted from her to the front doors that suddenly slid open.

Candice Proctor, Kevin's mom, and another woman walked into the store. Mrs. Proctor was talking loudly to the woman next to her. Her cheeks were bright red, and her hair looked windblown. An appearance I recognized. She was upset about something and wasn't shy about letting everyone around her know how she felt.

Instinct took over, and I dropped to the ground. I couldn't have Kevin's mom see me. She had to know that I'd left her son. No one could keep a secret when that woman was around. The truth involuntarily spilled out of you from one look. It was like her gaze held some magic truth serum.

I closed my eyes, praying that she didn't notice me. I had no idea what she was in here for, but there was no way I wanted to face her wrath—or her extremely passive-aggressive sighs and stares.

"Are you okay?"

I opened my eyes and glanced up to see Abigail peering down at me. She looked concerned.

"Do you need me to call an ambulance?" She pulled out her phone.

"Oh, no. No, I'm okay," I said, waving my hand. The last thing I needed was for her to call the paramedics. I wanted to stay hidden, not have a giant red arrow pointing down at me.

"Is she gone?"

Abigail glanced around. "Is who gone?"

"Mrs. Proctor."

An understanding expression passed over Abigail's face. She pulled out of my line of sight but then returned a few seconds later. "I don't see her. Did she come in here?"

I gingerly stood up. I brushed down my Godwin's Grocery apron before adjusting it over my clothes. "She came in right before I dropped down. She must be shopping now." I hesitantly looked around before I returned to pulling Abigail's items across the scanner.

"That's strange. I would have never imagined that woman shopping here." I glanced up at Abigail, whose face suddenly fell. "I mean, no offense. I didn't mean to say that..." She winced. "I'm an idiot."

I leaned closer to her. "It's okay. I know the family, and I agree. Godwin's seems a bit beneath her."

Relief flooded Abigail's expression. "Have you had run-ins with that family?"

I wasn't ready to share my life story with this woman, but I also felt a certain bond with her. She seemed nice, and the fact that she disliked the Proctor family endeared her to me.

"We have a history," I said with a smile.

Her eyes widened, but she gave me a knowing look. "That's the curse of living in a small town. History has a tendency to live on."

I blew out my breath. "Don't I know it."

I was down to the last few items to scan, so Abigail turned and grabbed her wallet from her purse. She removed her card and turned back to face me. "Are you free tomorrow night?" she asked as she tapped the edge of her card on the small shelf under the credit card machine.

"Tomorrow night?" I repeated.

She nodded. "I'm hosting a little get-together at my apartment. Some ladies from around town come over and we eat food and drink juice." She leaned forward. "Most of the time it's spiked." Her smile was soft and inviting. "You're totally welcome to come if you'd like."

I scanned her last item as I mulled over her words. It sounded nice, going out for the evening. Getting away from

Mom and her questioning stares. Or Dad and his insistence that she leave me alone.

But I wasn't sure if I was ready to fully immerse myself in this town again. And I wasn't ready to start wandering around where I could accidentally run into a Proctor unprepared and unarmed.

"I totally understand if you don't want to." Abigail's focus was on the credit card machine, but her cheeks were flushed. I hated that she seemed embarrassed that she even asked me.

I was being ridiculous. Hanging out with her wouldn't be a bad thing. If anything, I might feel some support from women my age. And right now, I needed all the support I could get.

"No, I want to," I said quickly, before she changed her mind and uninvited me.

Relief crossed her face. "Great! We meet at seven. Here's my number. Text me when you're off, and I'll send you my address." She handed me a business card.

I took it, glancing down at the card before reading it out loud. "The Shop Around the Corner?"

She nodded. "That's my bookstore-slash-bakery."

My register clocked her payment and spat out the receipt. I grabbed it and handed it to her. "Perfect. I'll text you."

She took the receipt and stuffed it into her purse. I grabbed a few of the full plastic bags and rounded the register to help her load up her shopping cart. She gave me a grateful smile before telling me that she'd see me tomorrow.

I told her I was looking forward to it before returning to my spot by the register. She got a phone call, gave me a quick wave, and brought her phone to her ear as she pushed the cart out of the store.

Now alone, I took in a deep breath. I couldn't help the smile that played on my lips as I stared at the checkout counter in front of me. I'd felt so alone for so long. I hadn't realized it at the time, but Kevin had isolated me from everyone. When I was with him, I had no friends and barely any contact with my family.

There was no such thing as a girls night out when I was with him. I lived to obey his commands. I went to his functions. Supported him when he needed it. I was just a prop for him. Someone on his arm to show off. That was, until he grew tired of me. Then I was a nuisance.

Tears pricked my eyes, but I angrily rubbed them away. I wasn't going to cry over him again. I was done with Kevin. I was never going to go back to him.

Ever.

I'd finally pulled myself together when movement to my right drew my attention, and my entire body froze. Standing at the entrance of the checkout was Mrs. Proctor and who I could only assume was her personal assistant. She was carrying bags of sugar.

I contemplated dropping down behind the counter again, but it didn't matter--Mrs. Proctor had already seen me. Her gaze was dark. Her eyes narrowed as she stared at me. Her lips drew into a tight line as she dragged her gaze up and down my body. I felt like I was a cow at auction, and she was determining if she wanted to bid.

"Juniper."

I blinked. Did someone just say my name?

"Juniper, it's time for your break. I can take over."

The world felt as if it were moving in slow motion. I turned to see Dad standing behind me. His expression was stoic, but there was a hint of urgency in his gaze. He wrapped his arm around my shoulder and guided me away from the register. "I'll take care of her. You just go into my office and wait there," he whispered in my ear.

My entire body felt numb, but with Dad's guidance, my feet started moving toward the stockroom door. I didn't stop until I was on the other side. The door swung shut behind me, and I hurried to Dad's office. I dropped down onto his desk chair and leaned forward to rest my arms on the solid oak top before I buried my face into the crook of my arm.

I wasn't sure how much time passed, but eventually, I heard the door open and the sound of my dad coming in. The door shut behind him, and he cleared his throat.

"She's gone," he said as he exhaled.

I sat up, certain that my forehead had a red mark on it from my forearm, but I didn't care. I was emotionally exhausted from seeing Mrs. Proctor.

"How did it go?" I whispered, not sure if I wanted to

hear his response. But I knew I couldn't focus until I found out.

He blew out his breath and raised his eyebrows. "She just asked me how long you've been back in town and then muttered something about Kevin not telling her. She didn't stick around long. She left all of the checkout stuff to Amelia, who I'm guessing is her assistant." He folded his arms across his chest. "She went outside, and from what I could see, she was pulling out her phone."

"Was she calling Kevin?" My voice sounded panicked, so I quickly pinched my lips shut. Sure, my parents were aware that my relationship with Kevin wasn't good, hence the black eye, but I don't think they realized how scared I was of him.

Dad studied me for a moment. "Do you think she'd call Kevin?" He stepped closer to me, and I could see he was gearing up to ask me more questions. Questions I wasn't ready to answer.

"Oh, no. I'm sure it was a work call. They were probably late for something." I shot him a forced smile before I stood. "Anyone manning the register? I should probably get out there." I walked around his desk and headed for the door.

"Juni."

Dad's nickname for me stopped me in my tracks. I closed my eyes for a moment, forcing myself to have more strength than I currently had. Dad cared about me. That was all.

He understood boundaries more than Mom did. He

wasn't going to pry, but he was going to show me that he cared.

I glanced at him from over my shoulder. He was standing behind his desk now with his readers perched on his nose.

"Yeah?" I asked, turning my body toward him but not letting go of the door handle.

"You know I'm here for you, right? You can tell me anything."

Guilt, anger, frustration with myself built up in my gut. I was a terrible daughter. I'd treated my family so badly, and now that I was back, I still couldn't bring myself to admit what had happened. To open up and let them in.

I was scared. It wasn't an excuse, but it was the truth. I just wasn't ready for the conversation that they wanted to have.

As if sensing my hesitation, Dad put his hands up in surrender and smiled. "Forget I said anything. Just know that I'm here and I love you."

His words washed over me, and for a moment, the burden that was crushing me felt a tiny bit lighter. Knowing he'd be there for me when I was ready did more for me than any conversation we could have where I told him everything.

The past was the past. There was nothing Dad or Mom or I could do to change it. I just wanted to focus on the future. On moving forward and becoming the new me.

Facing my history wouldn't do anything to rectify what had happened.

The best thing I could do for myself was to focus on where I was going.

"Thanks, Dad," I said, meeting his gaze one more time before turning the door handle and slipping out of his office.

I softly shut his door behind me and then shifted over to the wall and collapsed against it. I closed my eyes and tipped my head back. I inhaled through my nose and out my mouth a few times, trying to calm the nausea I was feeling.

I was just going to have to get used to seeing the Proctors around town. This was my first encounter; it was bound to go badly.

But I'd survived. I was going to feel stronger with each encounter until they no longer affected me like they did.

And until then, I was just going to have to pretend to be strong. Even if I didn't feel like it. I was good at faking a lot of things. I had to with Kevin. I was going to make it so no one around me would ever know of the pain I was carrying around.

7

CLAIRE

SWEET TEA & SOUTHERN GENTLEMAN

The pub was packed. It was 7pm, and it felt like half the town was inside Jax's little pub. He and Remus were at the bar, shouting orders and sliding beer bottles across the counter. On occasion, my gaze would drift over to him, but I really just kept to myself, trying to forget the morning's events.

We hadn't really talked since. When we did speak, it was just about what job he wanted me to do or the specifics on drink orders. I really had no interest in talking to Remus, and thankfully, Jax seemed to pick up on that and fielded all the conversations.

I'd been given the job of food runner for the cook, Henry. He was an older man who pulled his white hair back into a ponytail at the nape of his neck, and when he smiled, he had a few teeth missing.

He was thrilled that I was there to work with him. He

told me that I reminded him of his long-lost love, Yolonda, and when he spoke her name, that would instigate his trip down memory lane. Every time I went to the back to pick up an order, he'd start talking about one of their romantic trysts, and I would have to cut him short or the food would get cold. He'd wave me away, mumbling under his breath about how much he missed her. I'd grab the plates, setting them on a black tray, and push out into the pub.

I hated that I had to ask Jax for a place to stay and a job, but if I were honest with myself, I was enjoying the fast pace here. There wasn't time to sit down, which meant there wasn't time for me to think. Right now, my world was picking up food and delivering it to hungry customers.

It was just what I needed.

I pushed through the swinging doors to the kitchen to grab my next order. Henry was dishing up the fries, so I took a minute to slide the orders I'd just taken under the clip for Henry to grab.

"Busy night," I said once the food slips were in place.

Henry glanced up at me. "Huh?"

"It's a crazy night." I reached up and dabbed my forehead with the back of my wrist.

He shrugged as he turned his focus back to the food. "It's like this every night. Ever since the construction company came, we've been packed."

"Construction company?"

Henry nodded. "They wanted to buy the town up, but then decided it would be best to work with us instead of push us all out. Now they are offering grants to help people clean up their establishments." He slid a hamburger with steaming hot fries into the window before giving me a big smile. "I wonder if the boss is going to take one of those grants."

I glanced around at the kitchen. This place was outdated, and the appliances that Henry was working on looked like they could use an upgrade.

"Did Jax say he wasn't interested?"

Henry wiped his hands on his apron and shrugged. "Not in so many words. You know his grandfather was the one who opened this place. I just think he doesn't like things to change."

The wheels inside my head were turning. It would be foolish for Jax to turn down free money to fix up his place. It would help business. It wasn't that I thought Jax needed more money, but there had to be a time limit for applying. It would be foolish to let this opportunity pass him by.

Henry was studying me as I pulled myself from my thoughts and grabbed the order for table 4. I slipped the black tray up onto my shoulder and headed out of the kitchen.

I was a few steps into the main room when a particularly tipsy man tripped and nearly took me out. I spun, narrowly avoiding him. He stumbled forward and caught himself on a nearby stool.

"Craig!" Jax's voice could be heard above the music that was blaring on the jukebox and the constant hum of conversations around us. "You've had too much. I'm cutting you off."

Craig let out a low groan. "C'mon man," he slurred. "I'm a paying patron."

Jax walked closer to him, his gaze meeting mine before snapping over to Craig. "You almost took out my waitress." He tapped the counter. "You're done."

Realizing that I was still standing there with a tray of food on my shoulder, I snapped my attention back to the task at hand and made my way over to table 4. They were a rowdy bunch of guys. I'd never seen them before, and I'd just chalked it up to my absence. But after my conversation with Henry, I realized that they must be construction workers.

They were tan with scuffed hands and dirt under their fingernails. They were flirty, but I wasn't in the mood or the mindset to oblige.

"Food's here," I sang out as I started setting the dishes down on the table in front of them.

They all whooped and hollered as they leaned back so I could deliver the rest of the food. Suddenly, another man joined the group. He pulled out a chair, apologized for being late, and sat down. I recognized his sandy blond hair and eyes the color of the ocean. He watched me as I set the food down on the table like he recognized me too. When I moved to stand, he didn't drop his gaze, he just kept studying me until recognition passed through his gaze.

"It's you." He pointed his finger at me. "You were at the Apple Blossom B&B this morning."

Now I knew where I'd seen this man before. "You were the paramedic."

His smile widened, exposing a dimple on his left cheek. "That's right."

"Ooo, who is this?" one of his friends asked as he nudged him with his shoulder. "You out meeting girls again? I swear that ambulance is a chick magnet!" He met my gaze head-on. He was drunk; I could see it in his eyes. "It's the uniform."

The paramedic leaned closer to me. "You'll have to excuse my friends. They are a bunch of animals."

"Hey!" the guy sitting next to him protested before he punched the paramedic in the arm.

He winced and then waved to his friend. "See."

I slipped the black tray under one arm so it was no longer in the way and gave him a knowing smile. "It's okay. This is a bar." I leaned closer to him. "A place where inhibitions go to die."

He must have noticed that I leaned in because his eyes widened and his smile deepened, exposing a second dimple. "Name's Brett." He reached out his hand.

I knew I should just smile and walk away, but I didn't. Instead, like an alien had taken over my body, I reached out, grabbed his hand, and smiled back. "Claire."

He squeezed my hand. "Claire," he said like he was

enjoying the taste of my name on his tongue. "It's nice to meet you again."

"You, too."

I glanced down at our hands, realizing that he hadn't pulled back yet. His hand was warm and calloused, and it felt...nice.

He glanced down as well before he slowly—almost reluctantly—pulled his hand back. I met his gaze before turning to wait other tables.

"Have you worked here long?" he asked quickly, almost like he wanted me to stay.

I glanced over my shoulder. "Today is my first day."

"Really?"

I nodded. "So be kind."

He gave me a small salute. "Yes, ma'am."

I smiled and turned once more.

"When things slow down, care to join me for a game of pool?"

His question stopped my retreat. I faced him once more. I glanced over to the pool table that was currently occupied by a group of loud, drunk men. "I don't think they have any intention of giving up the table."

Brett glanced over to them and then back to me. "If I free the table, would you join me?"

I don't know why, but I glanced over at the bar and caught Jax staring. But as soon as I met his gaze, he dropped it back down to the man in front of him who was talking.

Jax's jaw muscles were set as if the man in front of him was making him mad.

"Unless you have a boyfriend."

I glanced back at Brett, who was watching Jax, too.

"I don't have a boyfriend," I whispered, hating that Jax still had this hold on me years later.

Brett smiled. "So, I'll see you at the pool table later?"

I had this feeling that if I didn't agree, he was just going to keep asking. I gripped the edge of the black tray and gave him a smile. "Sure."

It was like I'd given him the best birthday present. His eyes lit up, and he leaned back in his seat. "Perfect."

I gave him a quick nod before I hurried away from the table. Just as I passed by the bar, I glanced over at Jax. When our gazes met, he held mine for a moment before he turned back to take the drink order of a particularly busty woman flagging him down.

My heart was pounding as I pushed through the swinging doors. Henry wasn't around, so I took a moment to lean against the wall and take in some deep breaths. I set the tray down on the counter next to me and closed my eyes as I leaned forward.

I felt like I was on a Tilt-A-Whirl. I knew I wasn't with Jax, but flirting with another man made me feel like I was cheating on him. Especially when his cool, dark gaze was focused on me while I did it.

I was a mess.

"You feeling okay?" Henry's gravelly voice drew my

attention upward. He must have been in the freezer because he had an armful of frozen beef patties.

I quickly straightened and nodded before adjusting my apron and pushing the hair that had fallen around my face back up into my ponytail. "Yes, of course."

Henry paused as he studied me. "You're white as a sheet. Like you've seen a ghost."

I pinched my cheeks a few times and then gave him a big smile. "No ghost, and I'm just fine."

"You know, I don't want you getting people sick. Then people blame it on my cooking." He eyed me as he set the patties down on the grill. "I have a reputation to uphold."

"I feel perfectly fine. I'm not sick." I moved to the orders that were on deck and glanced over them.

"If you need to go home, I'm sure Jax will let you—"

"No. I'm fine." The last thing I wanted to do was talk to Jax. I was going to stay here and finish what I'd started.

Henry fell silent for a few seconds before he grunted and returned to flipping burgers. Since none of the orders I'd given him were finished, I grabbed my order pad and pushed back out to the pub. Just as I stepped past the doors, a foot jutted out, and suddenly the floor was rapidly coming at me.

I was too startled to scream. I flailed as I tried to grab onto anything that would keep me from landing hard on the cement floor.

Two warm hands grabbed onto my arms, and I was airborne. The hands turned into arms wrapping around me as I was pulled to a man's chest. My hands sprawled out on his chest, and all I could feel were the muscles underneath the familiar black t-shirt. My stomach sank when it fully registered that it was Jax holding on to me—tightly holding onto me.

"You need to be more careful," he growled, his lips dangerously close to my ear.

My lips parted, but no words came out. I wasn't sure what to say to him. My mind was screaming to push him away. That this was not good. But my heart was pumping at a speed I didn't know it could reach. All the senses in my body were going haywire, and I couldn't focus on any of them.

I felt him pull back. "Claire?"

"Um-hum," I said as I slowly met his gaze.

His eyebrows were drawn together, and he was searching my face. "Are you hurt?"

I slowly shook my head. "I think I'm okay."

His warm gaze turned icy as he dropped his arms and stepped back. He turned his focus to the ground. "You need to be more aware of your surroundings, Claire."

The sharpness of his voice made me feel as if I were a child getting a tongue-lashing from a parent. I wanted to fight back, but my entire body was still reacting to the feeling of his arms around me. I was oscillating between feeling cold in the absence of his body heat and warm from embarrassment and frustration with the way he was speaking to me.

"I'm sorry," was all I could manage.

He glanced over at me. "Your job is to take orders and then bring out the food. That's it."

I nodded. "I know that."

"I'm not paying you to flirt with drunks or Henry."

Heat began to prick my skin. What did he just accuse me of? Flirting with Henry? And I didn't make advances to Brett. He was the one who had talked to me. And why the hell did Jax even care? We weren't a couple. It had been years since we were.

Who flirted with me was no longer his to dictate.

I parted my lips to defend myself, but my brain couldn't form words. Instead, I just stood there, watching Jax give me one last scolding look before he returned to his spot behind the bar.

I narrowed my eyes at him, angry that he didn't wait so I could defend myself. I was frustrated that I'd allowed my body's reaction to his proximity to take all the good sense I had out of my head.

Realizing that I was just standing here, glaring, I reached up, pulled out my ponytail holder and shook out my hair. He didn't want me to flirt? Ha. I wasn't going to listen to him. I was a grown woman. I could do what I wanted, and there was nothing he could do about it.

I turned around and headed back over to the tables I had been waiting. I zeroed in on Brett. He must have noticed because his eyebrows went up and the look in his eyes turned to one of appreciation.

"Ready for me to dominate?" I asked as I set my hand next to him on the table and then rested on it. I leaned close.

A half smile played on his lips. "You want to dominate me?"

"I want you to regret ever asking me to play you at pool." I let my flirty smile emerge, and he responded just like I thought he would.

"Guys, I've got a game to play," he said to his friends, but his gaze never left mine.

A chorus of whoops and hollers filled the air as Brett pushed his chair back and stood. He kept close to me, his chest inches from mine. He was tall. Really tall. I hadn't noticed this morning, but I felt tiny in his presence.

He leaned down, his lips inches from my ear. It sent shivers across my skin. "Show me what you've got."

8

JAX

SWEET TEA &
SOUTHERN GENTLEMAN

My anger had reached an all-new level. It was like a burning fire in my gut that I couldn't put out no matter how hard I tried. I had no idea what Claire was doing, but I was pretty sure that playing pool with some drunk in my pub was the exact opposite of what I'd said I expected from her.

I wanted to go over to the pool table, shove that pool cue down the throat of the man standing *way* too close to Claire, and banish him from the pub. But I knew I couldn't do that. My butt would most certainly end up in prison, and I had a grandfather to help take care of.

No, if Claire wanted to play this game, I was going to keep my cool—even though it was taking all of my strength to do so.

Remus cleared his throat next to me. I glanced over to see him flick his gaze in Claire's direction. I didn't have to ask what he meant. He had *I told you so* written all over his face.

This was not a conversation I wanted to have with him. At least, not right now. I just shrugged as I filled a tumbler with ice. "He's a guest. She's keeping his friends here to drink, so we might as well take advantage," I said to Remus, who just quirked an eyebrow.

I guess this is what I get when I hire my ex-girlfriend and pay her with room and board. I was the idiot in this situation. I should have known better.

"Can I get a Coke?"

A soft, feminine voice rose over the boisterous conversations around the bar. I turned to see a woman with pale skin and curly red hair standing at the corner of the bar with her hands gingerly placed on top. She looked annoyed.

"A Coke?" I asked as I set the tumbler filled with ice on the counter and uncorked the bottle of whiskey next to it.

"Yes, please."

I nodded and returned the whisky bottle to the shelf behind me. "I think I can do that."

I grabbed a taller glass, filled it with some ice, and then pressed it against the soda tap. I let my gaze wander over to her. She was watching me with an expression of appreciation, and it bolstered my spirits. If Claire was going to flirt with some stranger, I could do the same.

I turned my charm on as I smiled at her. She met my gaze, her expression turning to one of surprise before she mirrored my smile.

"Are you new in town?"

She nodded. "I'm here with Deveraux Construction."

I finished filling up her glass. "The company that was trying to take over our town?" I asked as I set the soda in front of her.

Her eyes widened. "Well, I don't know about that. I'm just an architect. I'm here to advise on some new condos along the beach."

I rested my arms on the bar and leaned toward her. "An architect?" I repeated.

"Yes," she said.

I noticed that she didn't pull back. "So, are you here at my pub alone?"

She glanced around and then back to me. "This is your pub?"

I nodded and extended my hand. "Jax."

"Bailey." She slipped her hand into mine. It was petite and soft.

"Nice to meet you, Bailey."

"You too, Jax."

I held her hand a bit longer than normal before I let go and rested my hand on the counter. From the corner of my eye, I could just barely see Claire. She was facing me. I wanted to see if she was watching my interaction with Bailey, but I forced myself to stay focused. I didn't want Claire to know I was thinking about anyone but the woman currently in front of me.

"You didn't answer my question about friends." I glanced to either side of her. "Or a boyfriend."

"You never asked about a boyfriend." Her cheeks flushed as her gaze softened. "You just asked if I was here alone."

"I didn't? I swear I did."

She bit her bottom lip and shook her head. "No and no."

"No?"

She nodded.

I grabbed her glass of Coke. "Where are you sitting?" I walked to the edge of the bar and then made my way toward her. "I'm more than happy to deliver this to your table."

She fell in step with me. "Oh. That's so nice." Then she waved to a small bar-height table near the back...right next to where Claire was playing pool. "I'm right there."

"Perfect." I led the way and set the glass down on the table.

She climbed up onto the stool and rested her hands on the table. She glanced around and then back to me. "What about you? Any girlfriend?"

My gaze drifted to the pool table, which was now just a few feet away. Claire was hunched over it trying to line up a shot, and the guy she was with had his arms around her as if he was *helping* her. Anger ignited in my gut again, so I turned back to Bailey.

I needed to push Claire from my mind. I needed to stop caring about what she was doing or who she was talking to. I was free. Claire was free. And this was good for me. It was helping squelch any thoughts of me and Claire getting back together.

It was a torturous kind of aversion therapy.

"No girlfriend, totally free." I gave her a half smile that I knew made women melt.

"Oh," she said as she slowly nodded. "So, you're unattached, and I'm unattached..." She pointed her finger at me and then to herself. "Maybe two unattached people should get dinner sometime?"

I liked a forward woman. I played so many games with Claire when we were teens, that she had me running in circles. It was nice to talk to someone who actually knew what she wanted and went for it.

"Dinner?" I asked. "Do you have a place in mind?" Then I leaned forward. "Not here. I try not to mix business and pleasure."

She blushed. "I just got to Harmony. Your place is the only place I know."

"Ah." I shoved my hands into the front pockets of my jeans. "Well, there's the diner. We could go there. It's not a five-star restaurant, but it serves good food."

"The diner?" Her eyebrows rose. "Sounds good to me."

"Friday night?"

Her smile was soft and inviting. "I can do that."

"Great." I reached out my hand. "Can I get your phone number?"

She nodded and adjusted her purse so she could dig around inside. She emerged with her phone and handed it to me. I sent myself a text from her phone and then handed it back to her. She took it and slipped it back into her purse before pulling out her wallet.

"I should pay you for the Coke."

I reached out and rested my hand on hers. "Consider it on the house." I let my hand linger, and her gaze slowly went from our hands to my face. "Thanks," she whispered in a tone that would make any man go wild.

I pushed aside the fact that it seemed to have no effect on me and just smiled. "Of course." I pulled my hand back. "Let me know if you need anything else," I said as I rocked back on my heels.

"Will do."

I shot her one last smile before I started to turn back toward the bar. Halfway around, my gaze caught Claire's. She was watching me, her eyes hooded and her gaze dark. She had no expression on her face, so I couldn't read what she was thinking, but my entire body responded to the fact that she was paying attention.

I met her gaze, gave her a quick smile and a wink before I turned my focus back to Remus and the thirsty patrons waiting for a refill.

My mind was a muddled mess when I got back behind the bar. An empty tumbler got shoved into my hand, so I focused on filling it back up with some vodka.

"What was that?" Remus' voice drew my attention over.

"What was what?"

Remus shot me a *you can't lie to me* look.

I shrugged as I handed the now full tumbler to the customer who tossed a ten on the bar and left before I could get him his change. "I'm just being hospitable."

Remus snorted. "I've never seen you deliver anything, much less a Coke."

"Maybe I'm trying to up my game. You know this place runs on return customers." I shrugged. "Is it a crime to be nice?"

Remus paused from washing the glasses in the sink and turned. "Not a crime to be nice. But it's an effort in futility if you're only being nice to make your ex jealous."

I scoffed as I shifted my gaze around the bar. I needed a second to calculate how I was going to respond to his accusations. He always seemed to know when I was lying, and I was in no way mature enough to get called on my crap right now. I felt like my chest was cracked open, and my heart was exposed to everyone around me.

"Wasn't trying to make her jealous. Besides, from the looks of things, she didn't even notice with that tree trunk hanging around her." Good. This was good. My voice was calm as I talked about the guy who was currently tucking Claire's hair behind her ears. "Is she the only one who can move on?" Without realizing it, I waved toward the pool table.

Remus followed my gesture, but he didn't look convinced when he brought his focus back to me. His smile was irritating me in a way that it had never bothered me in the past.

Why wouldn't he believe me? "I've moved on," I said before I could police my words. In all my life, someone saying they'd moved on just proved that they had, in fact, not moved on.

I growled and turned toward the guy who was standing next to the bar, waiting for me to take his order. "What?" I barked out.

He raised his eyebrows, but I just shrugged it off. I wasn't in the mood for any of this.

"Can I get a whiskey?"

I nodded, grabbed the twenty from his hand, and opened the cash register. Once he had his change and drink in hand, he left the bar and I turned back to Remus. I'd finally worked out a response in my brain that didn't make me sound like an idiot.

"Listen, I know I haven't really dated since Claire. My relationships never last very long—"

"You wear the ring you wanted to give her around your neck."

Heat pricked at my cheeks from his words. He was right, but I hated that he knew this about me. I'd confessed it to him one drunken night when we stayed late after the pub closed. I barely remembered that I'd told him the next morning, but he'd never let me live it down since.

"And that," I said through gritted teeth.

He smirked. He loved to goad me.

"But that doesn't mean I'm still hooked on her. I'm

just..." I paused to think of the right word. "I'm just nostalgic."

He finished rinsing a glass and shut off the water before he turned to face me with a dish towel in hand. "Um, okay," he said.

"It's true."

He wiped the sides of the tumbler down, and from the way he was studying his movements, he was contemplating his words. He sighed as he set down the dry tumbler next to the other clean ones. He hung the dish towel next to the sink and then turned to face me. "You know I'm not the one you have to convince." He folded his arms and leaned one hip against the counter next to him.

I scowled. "You are very much the person I have to convince."

He shook his head. "There's only one person you have to convince that you've moved on."

"Oh, really. And who is that?"

A man shouted his drink order from the other side of the bar, so Remus nodded in his direction as he pushed off the counter. He paused next to me before glancing down. "You."

9

CLAIRE

SWEET TEA & SOUTHERN GENTLEMAN

T his was not what I expected. Brett was actually nice. Sure, the reason I'd agreed to play pool with him was because I was angry at Jax—which I'm not saying was the right thing to do—but after ten minutes of talking and laughing with Brett, I was beginning to relax for the first time since I got back to Harmony.

Brett was simple. He grew up on a ranch in Montana. He was saving up so he could go back and invest in some land. He was wholesome and uncomplicated. Right now, that seemed perfect for me. Especially since I was trying with all my might not to let my gaze wander over to Jax and the girl he'd brought over to flirt with.

Jax was about as subtle as a bull in a china shop. He thought he was smooth and stealthy, but he wasn't. His smile was too big while he listened to what she was saying, and he leaned in a bit too close when he talked. He was interested in this girl, but not in the way that most guys would be interested in her.

He was using her to make me jealous, which meant me flirting with Brett had an effect on him. Good. It should.

"What about you? You listened to me go on and on about my future plans, do you have any?"

I pulled my attention away from Jax and his sad attempt at flirting and focused on Brett. "Would you think badly of me if I say I don't have a plan?"

He was rubbing chalk on the end of his pool cue. His gaze met mine, and he smiled, his genuine half smile. *Take notes, Jax. This is how you make a woman swoon.* "I don't think anyone could think badly of you."

My gaze darted over to Jax and then back to Brett. "You'd be surprised."

Brett set down the chalk block and glanced around, puffing out his chest. "Show me which man would speak ill of thee, fair maiden, and I will defend your honor."

I laughed and swatted at his arm. "He's not here," I lied. "And it's no one in particular, just...all of my exes."

Ever since Jax, I'd struggled to form any sort of meaningful bond. Sure, I dated other guys, but they never lasted long. I always broke up with them before they could hurt me —or my mother found out and called to tell me their entire history that she'd looked up on the internet.

Protecting a man from my mother was priority one. The last thing I needed was for them to meet the woman who gave birth to me and wonder if that was what they had in store if they sealed the deal with me.

"It's my gain, then."

The sudden warmth of his fingertips on my elbow drew my attention over. I hadn't noticed him getting closer. He was standing inches from me with a softness to his gaze that made my body feel as if I'd drunk an entire mug of hot chocolate.

"Thanks," I said, glancing up at him through my eyelashes.

He grinned and then handed me the pool cue he'd been working on and took the one that I was currently holding. "Now, don't think your pretty face and soft voice is going to distract me. I do plan on wiping the floor with you."

I scoffed and began to circle the table. "Oh really." I contemplated my move, assessing where each ball lined up with the cue ball. I found a striped ball that was close to the left far pocket, so I leaned over the table to line up the shot. The cue ball ricocheted off the striped ball, and the sound of the ball landing safe in the pocket had me cheering.

"That's one for me," I said as I poked his chest with my finger.

Brett feigned pain as he clutched his hand to his chest and raised his fist in the air. "I will conquer," he said as he grabbed his pool cue and started circling the table.

I was so distracted with Brett that I almost didn't notice Jax get up from his spot with the redhead and move back over to the bar. I watched her watch Jax as he retreated. Her smile made my stomach churn, and the way she blew out her breath as she glanced down at the table and traced the grain lines in the wood had my entire body heating.

I was annoyed that she liked him. She wasn't supposed to like him. And I wasn't sure *why* she wasn't supposed to like him.

"You okay?"

I snapped my attention over to Brett, who was walking up to me. I quickly shook off my feelings about Jax and his mystery girl and focused back on the game. "Yeah, totally."

He glanced toward the bar. "Is that your boss?"

I followed his gaze and saw Jax talking to Remus. Jax looked annoyed, and Remus looked amused. That pretty much summed up their relationship.

"Kind of. He owns this place."

"Ah," Brett glanced down at me. "Do you think he's okay with you playing pool instead of waiting tables?"

I shrugged. "We kind of have a bartering deal right now. He's not really paying me."

Brett looked confused. "Bartering deal?"

I nodded as I turned my focus back to the game. "Yeah. We grew up together. He's doing me a favor, and in exchange, I agreed to help out here." I saw an option and lined my pool cue up to strike.

"You grew up together?" There was hesitation in his voice, and I knew what he was going to ask before the words even left his lips.

"It's over. We haven't spoken in years. I'm only here

because my mom had surgery and the woman who practically raised me is in the hospital. His was the only place for me to stay."

"You're living with him?"

My mind was so muddled that I couldn't think straight. I liked talking to Brett. He made me forget my mom and the messed-up history I had here. But from the sound of his voice, it seemed he was realizing my life might be more than he wanted to handle.

"Just for a few days. I needed a place to stay." I gave Brett a smile. But I knew things had already gone south, and there was no way I was going to be able to fix it. I set the pool cue down on the table and turned to face him. "I should really get back to work."

Brett looked confused, but he didn't ask me to stay. Instead, he just nodded, and I gave him one final smile before I turned and walked toward the kitchen. Henry wasn't happy that I'd been gone for ten minutes, so after a quick tongue-lashing from him, I washed my hands and returned to delivering plates to customers.

I kept away from Brett and from Jax. I was exhausted and ready for this night to be over. Henry left at ten, and once he was gone, I didn't have much to do besides bus tables and wipe them down. I lingered in the back, listening to an audiobook on my phone, and every so often, I'd peek out to see if there was anything for me to take care of.

Remus left at 1:30. The pub closed at two. He didn't say anything to me as he pushed through the swinging doors and walked past. I heard his locker slam and then the back door open. and he was gone.

I sat on an old, fraying barstool, resting my cheek on my hand. My elbow was propped up next to the food counter that Henry had wiped clean. I closed my eyes, only to be jolted awake from the feeling of falling. I set my arm down and straightened my posture in an effort to wake up.

Realizing that I was only going to fall asleep again if I stayed sitting, I slipped off the barstool and made my way over to the swinging doors. I peeked through the small window at the top to see that, besides one or two customers, the place was empty. I couldn't see Jax, but I could see a bunch of empty beer bottles and tumblers, so I grabbed a nearby grey tub and pushed through the doors.

The sooner I got this place cleaned up, the sooner I was going to be able to go home.

I busied myself with dumping the garbage in the nearby trash can and stacking the empty glass tumblers into the grey tub. Movement by the bar drew my attention over. Jax was shaking the shoulders of Mr. Smith, my old seventh-grade teacher.

Mr. Smith had passed out on the bar, and Jax was trying to revive him. It took some effort, but eventually, Jax had him sitting up. Jax wrapped Mr. Smith's arm around his shoulders and then used his side to help stabilize the man as he pulled him to standing. Mr. Smith muttered something under his breath, and Jax responded in a calm voice.

With his arm now wrapped around Mr. Smith's waist,

Jax started leading him to the front door. Mr. Smith took a step and then a second step before his legs gave out and he started to sink to the floor. Jax was desperately trying to keep him on his feet, but Mr. Smith's sudden shift of weight caused Jax to lose his grip.

I set the grey tub down on a nearby table and hurried over. As soon as I got to them, I grabbed onto Mr. Smith's free arm and wrapped it around my shoulders. "Come on, Mr. Smith. Your wife won't be happy if you spend the whole night here."

The jostling of Jax and I trying to stand Mr. Smith up seemed to sober him enough to plant his feet underneath him.

"Claire?" Mr. Smith asked, blowing his alcohol breath over me.

"Long time no see, Mr. Smith," I said as I wrapped my arm around his waist, brushing Jax's arm in the process.

Up until this moment, Jax had kept his gaze forward. But now, his gaze snapped to me and there was a look in his eyes that I couldn't quite read, and I was pretty sure I didn't want to try to dissect it.

I was just trying to help. He had to see that.

Mr. Smith mumbled something about his wife leaving him, but I was too busy keeping his feet moving and handling the weight of his body pressing down on me to try to listen. Jax and I got him through the front door, where a ride share was waiting. Jax leaned forward and opened the door, and we worked together to get Mr. Smith in the car enough for us to buckle him in.

I wasn't sure what to do, so I just waited as Jax moved to the rolled down window of the passenger door to talk to the driver. The driver was concerned about vomit, but Jax brushed his concern off as he reached into his back pocket and pulled out his wallet. Then he handed the driver a few twenties and stepped back.

The car peeled out of the parking lot a few seconds later, his lights disappearing into the distance.

I wrapped my arms around my chest, holding my upper arms with my hands to warm them up. Jax didn't turn around right away. Instead, he lingered on the sidewalk, staring in the direction the ride share car had gone. I wanted to ask him if something was wrong, but I decided to keep quiet.

"Thanks for your help," Jax finally said as he turned around.

My gaze followed him, but he didn't look up to meet it. He passed by me, walked over to the front door, and held it open.

"Of course. I figured you didn't want him staying the night. And there was no way you were going to be able to get him out of here yourself."

He let out a soft humph as I passed by him into the pub. I glanced over to see him staring at the ground. "I could have handled him myself," he said as he followed after me, letting the door shut behind him.

"Eh, didn't look like it." I shrugged.

Jax stopped and glanced over at me. "Who do you think carts him out of the pub every time he overdrinks? Me." He stepped closer. "And who does it all by himself every time?" He was inches from me now. "Me."

My gaze was focused on his chest. A lot had changed in the years since I moved away. He was no longer the tall, slender guy I used to date. He'd definitely filled out. His shoulders were broad. His chest was defined. And his arms looked like he could carry Mr. Smith and me at the same time.

"It's okay to admit that sometimes you need help," I said, my voice soft as I slowly drew my gaze up to meet his.

He was staring down at me. His eyes dark and his brows drawn together. He looked in pain. Did it frustrate him that much that I didn't think he could have brought Mr. Smith out on his own? He had to know that I was partly joking.

"That's the thing. I don't need help." He took a step back. "You need help. That's why you came to me. That's why I let you work here." He turned and headed back to the bar.

Heat pricked at my skin as I followed after him. I was mad. "Well, if your dog hadn't impregnated my dog, we wouldn't be in this situation. I'd be able to live at the B&B..." My voice drifted off as I realized what I'd started to say.

But Jax picked up on it. He knew I was lying, and I hated that. "Oh, living with me is worse than with your mom." He scoffed as he turned on the faucet next to him and began to rinse out a dishcloth. "That's rich."

I hated that this man knew so much about me. I couldn't tell white lies when I was around him because he would pick up on them. And he would always have something to say in response.

"Well, you're both stubborn and stuck in your ways," I retorted as I marched over to pick up the grey tub that I'd set down earlier. I rested it on my hip as I started to move around the pub once more.

"Ha! I'm stuck in my ways?" He was wiping the counter vigorously. I wasn't sure if it was that dirty or if he was just trying to work off some frustration.

"You're the definition of someone stuck in their ways." I set the tub down again, so I could start ticking examples off on my fingers. "You won't let people help you. You're stubborn. You still wear the same ridiculous screen-printed t-shirts you did in high school." I paused and looked at him. "And I'm pretty sure you still eat two eggs with toast when you think a cold is coming on. Like that does something." I mumbled the last sentence under my breath.

He stopped moving and was staring at me now. "How about how you don't let people help you. You flirt with every guy you see. You hold your breath when we pass by a cemetery, and you kiss your fingers and touch the top of the car when you drive through a yellow light like it's magic and will make all of your dreams come true."

I turned to face him head-on. "I do let people help me." I

waved toward him. "Asking for help is the first step, which I did. I do not flirt with every guy, and it just makes sense to hold your breath when you drive by a cemetery." My frustration had me sweating, so I reached up and started to pull my hair into a ponytail. "And what's so wrong about making a wish? They never hurt anyone."

"You don't flirt with every guy?" He rounded the corner and took a step closer to me. "What were you doing with that guy earlier?" He waved toward the pool table where Brett and I had played a game.

He had noticed. And it had bothered him. That was another tally for me.

And then the image of him flirting with the redhead flashed through my mind. I wasn't going to go down for flirting when he did the exact same thing. "And what about the girl you were flirting with over at that table?" I motioned toward the table he'd lingered at a little too long.

"I was just delivering her order." He folded his arms across his chest.

"You were leaning a little too close for just an innocent encounter." I placed my hands on my hips and glared at him. "Maybe you should look in the mirror before you come for me."

He studied me. His gaze was dark, like he was battling something inside of himself. Then he dropped his arms and shoved a hand into his back pocket. He pulled out a folded-up piece of paper and handed it to me. "Here."

I took it from him and stared down at it. "What is this?"

"Your Prince Charming left this for you earlier."

"Prince Charming?" I started to unfold the piece of paper and glanced down at it. Brett had written his name and number along with a note that said, *I'm not sure what happened, but I hope to see you again.*

I smiled at the note. It was sweet that he still wanted to talk to me even though I'd lost my mind when I was talking to him. My emotions had definitely gotten the best of me, and Brett didn't seem bothered.

He really was a nice guy.

Movement in front of me drew my gaze up. Jax had moved back behind the counter. His jaw muscles were tense, and he kept his attention focused on cleaning up behind the bar. He didn't look over at me. He looked so unreachable, that I slipped Brett's number into my pocket and returned to cleaning the tables.

Jax and I worked in silence until the pub was picked up and the tables and countertops were wiped down. Then he turned off the light and pushed through the swinging door to the back hallway.

We didn't speak as he locked up, and neither of us spoke a word to each other as he drove to his house. After he parked, he took off to the back porch and then disappeared inside.

I didn't go in right away. Instead, I found Carmel snuggled up in the few old blankets he'd given me to make her a bed in the garage. I scratched behind her ears a few times, planted a kiss on her head, and thanked her for always being excited to see me.

Then I made my way across Jax's yard and up his porch steps. When I got into the kitchen, only the light above the sink was on. I got a glass of water and brought it into Jax's guest room, shutting the door behind me.

I needed a shower, but I was too tired. So I just slipped off my clothes, put on a pair of pajamas, and climbed into bed.

I quickly put Brett's number into my phone and then set my phone on the nightstand. I tossed and turned a few times as I tried to fall asleep. For some reason, I couldn't quite get Jax's expression out of my head. The one he'd had when he handed me Brett's number.

But eventually, I pushed any thought of Jax and his pained expression from my mind as darkness overtook me, and I fell asleep.

10

JAX

SWEET TEA &
SOUTHERN GENTLEMAN

I stupidly thought that a good night's sleep would help fix my sour mood. I was wrong. I dropped into bed last night thinking all I needed was a solid eight hours to remove the image of Claire's smile as she unfolded that man's note.

It was the first thing I saw when I woke up, and no matter how hard I pushed myself at the gym, it refused to leave my head.

The man she'd flirted with while working at *my* pub wanted to see more of her, and Claire seemed to want the same. I knew it shouldn't bother me, but it did. I hated that other men looked at her. She deserved so much more than to be eye candy to some guy who wasn't going to treat her like...

My thoughts were going into uncharted territory. If I didn't stop now, I was going to confess something to myself that I wasn't ready for. It was best for me to stop thinking and just get on with my day.

I slipped into a pair of grey sweatpants and a white t-shirt and pushed my hand through my damp hair, spraying the last bits of water from my hair. I pulled open my bedroom door and headed to the kitchen to make myself some coffee.

Gramps was sitting at the table with a mug of coffee and today's newspaper spread out in front of him. I nodded in his direction but didn't say anything as I pulled open the cupboard door to grab a coffee filter and started making myself a pot. Once the hum of the machine filled the silent air, I focused on making some eggs and bacon for breakfast.

"Want me to make some food for you?" I asked Gramps while holding up the eggs and bacon.

He glanced over his readers at me and nodded. "Yes, please."

I headed over to the stove, where I pulled out two pans and turned the burners on. I whisked the eggs while the butter melted and the bacon began to crackle in the heat.

"What about our guest?"

I turned, mid-whisk, to Gramps, who had put his mug down and was sitting back in his chair with his arms crossed. "Guest?" I asked out of instinct before it sunk in who he was talking about. "You mean Claire?"

"Do we have another guest that I don't know of?" He raised his eyebrows and nodded at me.

Sure, there was a time or two where I brought a girl

home, but they never came back again. From the incredulous look on Gramps' face, he was implying more than made me comfortable.

"No," I said as I turned to the now sizzling pan of butter and dumped the whisked eggs into it. It snapped and popped as the eggs spread across the hot surface. I dumped the bowl into the sink and wiped my hands on a nearby dish towel. I turned to face him, but he was no longer staring at me. Instead, he was pushing against the tabletop like he had somewhere to be.

"I'll do it," I grumbled, hating that he was forcing me to go talk to Claire. But I didn't want him to be the one to do it. I wasn't sure what he would say to her. Most days, Gramps had all his faculties. But there were a few times—and they were getting more frequent—that Gramps would forget where he was or who I was.

The last thing I needed was for him to have an episode in front of Claire. If I was going to maintain my sanity, I was going to have to keep Claire as far away from me and my business as I possibly could.

Gramps nodded and returned to his seat. He pulled the paper back up, disappearing behind it. I brushed my hands down my shirt and turned the corner, heading in the direction of my guest room. I raised my hand to knock, and I froze.

I was moments away from staring into the eyes of the girl who broke my heart. Years ago, when she dumped me out of the blue, and last night, when she flirted with some stranger she didn't know.

Why was I the idiot who couldn't seem to move on? Why was I the only one who seemed to be holding onto what we had? Claire had moved on. She'd left town. Started a life without me. Why couldn't I get it through my thick skull that she wanted someone else?

"'Cause you're an idiot," I murmured under my breath.

"Did you need something?"

Claire's voice made me jump back. My heart was pounding a million miles a minute. I whipped my gaze to her. She was standing in front of me with a towel wrapped around her hair and another wrapped around her body. She had her hands tucked firmly under her arms as if she feared that her towel would suddenly malfunction and drop to the floor.

Heat permeated my entire body as that thought entered my mind, and I pushed it out before it took root. Hoping that she didn't see my reaction to her, I cleared my throat.

"You startled me," I squeaked out.

Claire raised her eyebrows and glanced around. "I'm sorry." Then she turned her focus back to me. "You *are* standing in front of my door."

I glanced toward the wood door. I shoved my hands into my front pockets and nodded. "Right."

"So, do you—"

"Jax! The food!"

Gramp's panicked voice from the kitchen snapped me

out of the awkward haze that seeing Claire had put me in, and my entire body moved. "Just seeing if you wanted some breakfast," I called over my shoulder as I ran to the kitchen.

"Oh."

I heard her response, but I didn't wait for her to finish. Instead, I rushed into the kitchen to find Gramps holding both pans above the stove. Smoke filled the room with the smell of burnt eggs and bacon.

I swore under my breath as I took the pans from Gramps and headed to the back door. Once outside, I made my way into the woods and dumped the food behind a tree. I glanced at the damage, and it wasn't good. I might as well throw away the pans. There was no way I was going to salvage them.

I leaned my head back and tipped my face up toward the sky. The morning rays from the sun washed over me. I took in a deep breath as I tried to calm my mind. I was going to go insane if I kept this up. I needed to get my head on straight and push Claire from my mind.

I needed a moment of peace where I could build up a wall so high around my heart that I would never look at Claire as anyone other than someone from my past. I just needed a minute to breathe.

Realizing that I must look ridiculous, standing in my backyard, holding two damaged pans, and tipping my face toward the sky, I rolled my shoulders and headed back to the house. I tossed the pans in the nearby trash can and took the back porch steps two at a time.

Gramps had returned to his seat, and Claire was dressed in a dark pair of jeans and a baby blue shirt. She was getting a glass of milk when I walked back into the kitchen. Gramps was drinking his coffee and was eyeing me from over the mug. From the look in his eye, he was wondering if everything was okay.

"Breakfast is ruined," I said as I made my way over to the kitchen sink and turned it on.

"Oh," Claire said as she returned the milk jug to the fridge and turned around to face me. She leaned against the counter and took a sip of her milk. "That's okay. I was going to go see Rose today. She's expecting me."

I nodded. "Okay." Good. Get her out of the house.

She drank her milk in silence. I wasn't sure what to say, and Gramps had returned to reading his paper. With her glass now empty, Claire made her way over to the sink and rinsed it out. She set the glass in the sink and turned around.

"Thing is," she said slowly.

I raised my eyebrows.

She tucked her hands into her front pockets. "I was hoping you could give me a ride since my car died yesterday." She offered me a small shrug, but then winced, her hand going up to her neck as she cradled it.

I'd seen her do this a few times, but she'd just shrugged it off like it was nothing. But now I was beginning to wonder if it *was* something and she just wasn't saying anything. She must have noticed me studying her because she instantly dropped her hand down to rest on the counter.

I glanced at the clock. I needed her gone, but I didn't think it would happen like this. I couldn't be in the same house with her, much less my truck. Trading my home for a smaller space with no rooms sounded like torture.

"Why don't you just take my truck?" I offered as I moved to the little dish by the door and grabbed my spare key. I crossed the kitchen and tucked it into Claire's hand.

She stared down at the key and then slowly raised her gaze to meet mine. "And what will you drive?"

I waved my hand toward Gramps. "I'll borrow Gramps' truck."

"No, you won't. I've got a doctor's appointment at noon. Your aunt Pricilla is going to drive it for me."

I frowned, hating that Gramps wasn't working with me on this. If telepathy was a thing, I'd be saying a lot of words to him right now. "Well, I just..." My voice drifted off with my excuse. I had nothing. I might as well accept that I wasn't going to get out of taking Claire to the medical center.

The sound of a phone ringing distracted me. I glanced over to Claire, who was pulling her phone from her pocket. She frowned as she stared at the screen but then swiped and lifted her phone to her ear. "Hello?"

Not wanting to stand in the kitchen and watch her talk on the phone, I busied myself with trying to find something to eat in the cupboard.

"Hey, Abigail."

So, Abigail was calling her. Relief flooded my body. It

wasn't Brett. Had she even called him? Probably. I shook my head. That's not what I should be thinking about.

Deep in the back of the pantry, I found a box of granola bars and pulled them out. I wasn't sure how long they'd been back there, and I really didn't care. They were food, and I needed sustenance.

"Tonight? Sure. That sounds like fun." Then Claire paused, and I felt her gaze on me. "Actually, I'm working at the pub with Jax, so I don't think I'll be able to come."

Having Claire not work with me tonight sounded like just the break I needed. "You can go," I said with my mouth full of the granola bar. It came out muffled and with a few bits of food, but I wasn't going to miss this opportunity to have her gone.

Claire drew her brows together to ask me if I was sure. I nodded as I crossed the kitchen and grabbed a glass of water. These bars were old and dry, like sawdust in my mouth.

"Jax says he doesn't need me. So, I'll be there. What time?" Abigail paused. "Seven. That works." Then she pinched the bridge of her nose between her fingers. "Any chance you could give me a ride? My car is on the fritz."

I thought about offering to give her a ride, but I wasn't going to be available, so I silently prayed that Abigail could pick her up.

"Perfect. I'll see you at six thirty." She paused. "Wonderful. Talk to you later." She hung up the phone and slipped it into her pocket. Her gaze made its way over to me, and she offered me a soft smile. "I guess Abigail is having a girls night at her house, and she invited me."

"Wonderful." It came out a bit too loud and a bit too enthusiastic. Claire looked startled, and Gramps was staring at me from over his newspaper. I cleared my throat and clapped my hands before rubbing my palms together like I was trying to warm them up. "It's just hard not to have friends. I'm glad that some of the ladies in town are reaching out to you." I glanced between Claire and Gramps. "Am I wrong?"

Claire shook her head, and Gramps just chuckled as he returned to the paper. "It's not wrong. You just sounded like you were really excited to get rid of me." She narrowed her eyes.

The stress of the last twenty-four hours was slowly being peeled off my shoulders. In no time, Claire was going to be busy, and I was going to get a break from my confusing feelings for her. I was excited for a break—but that didn't mean I wanted her to leave again.

I just...needed some time to breathe.

Not wanting to respond to Claire's comment—that woman had a way of seeing right through my answers—I shoved my hands into my front pockets and shrugged. "Should we get going? Visiting hours start soon, right?"

Claire glanced at the clock above the oven and nodded. "You're right. We should get going." She started to move past before she stopped and glanced over at me. "Thanks for giving me a ride."

The way she looked up at me had my heart racing, and the look on her face was genuine. I loved and hated it at the same time.

"Sure," I whispered.

She held my gaze for a moment longer before she offered me a soft smile and headed out of the kitchen. I stood there unable to move. There was something about her being so close to me. The way she looked up at me. All I wanted to do was wrap my arms around her and kiss her. And I hated that.

"Shouldn't you get moving?" Gramps' question broke through my thoughts, and suddenly I could move again.

I glanced over at him. He had a knowing look on his face. He was the only other person besides Claire who had the uncanny ability to see right through me.

"Yeah, yeah," I said as I turned and headed after Claire.

Thankfully, the ride to the medical center was quiet. Claire spent the entire time staring out the window, and I kept both hands on the steering wheel, trying to relax my hands because my knuckles were turning white and my fingers were cramping. I pulled into the visitor's parking lot and into the nearest open spot.

As soon as I pushed my truck into park, Claire glanced over at me. "Are you coming with?" she asked.

I hesitated before I nodded. Even though things were strained between me and Claire, I adored Rose. She had always been so supportive of my relationship with Claire, even though Claire didn't have the same loyalty. I wanted to make sure Rose was okay and let her know that I was thinking about her.

Claire studied me before she grabbed the door handle and pulled. I did the same. Once my feet were on the ground, I slammed the door. We walked side by side through the parking lot, up onto the sidewalk, and through the sliding front doors. The lobby was busy with people standing at the front desk or sitting in chairs that dotted the waiting room.

I stayed behind Claire as she waited in line for the next available receptionist. Once she was called up to the desk, I waited off to the side as Claire talked. She nodded a few times and then thanked the receptionist before joining me.

She didn't look up as she said, "Room 104, this way."

I followed her through the doors the receptionist opened for us. Claire didn't say anything as she walked down the hall, ticking off room numbers as she went.

When we got to room 104, she knocked, and a faint voice called, "Come in."

Claire grabbed the handle but then looked back at me. "I should make sure that she's decent," Claire said before stepping inside.

I nodded and moved away from the door. I didn't want to see Rose if she wasn't decent any more than I was sure Rose would. I waited in the hallway, nodding toward the nurses who were eyeing me as they walked by. It felt like an eternity before Rose's door opened and Claire was standing there.

"You can come in now."

I hesitated, but when Claire stepped to the side, I took that as my opening and walked into the room. Rose was sitting on the bed when I cleared the curtain. Her eyes lit up when she saw me, and her signature smile spread across her face.

"Jax," she said as she lifted her arms and motioned for me to hug her.

I obliged, reveling in her familiar hug. She had a way of making all your worries melt away. She held me for a few seconds before she pulled back. "I was so excited when Claire told me that you were here to see me," she said before offering me a wicked smile. "It's nice to see the two of you together in the same room again."

I glanced over at Claire, who shook her head. "I was thinking about grabbing some breakfast from the cafeteria. Can I grab you anything?" Claire held her gaze on Rose.

Rose waved away her question but kept her gaze on me. "I'm fine. They brought me breakfast this morning."

From the corner of my eye, I saw Claire glance over at me. "Do you want to help me get some food?"

Rose reached out and grabbed my hand. "Why don't you go and get some food? I'll stay here and catch up with Jax."

I glanced up at Claire, who looked like she was in the middle of an internal battle. She didn't have to speak for me to know what the problem was. She didn't want to leave me alone with Rose, but she didn't know how to say those words.

Because then she'd have to give a reason for why she didn't want me and Rose to talk. Even though everyone in this room knew the reason would be our history. Which meant she remembered what we once had as vividly as I did.

Her desire to save face must have won out because she let out a sigh and headed out the door. The sound of the handle engaging filled the silent air and must have been the signal Rose was waiting for.

Her gaze snapped to me. "Have a seat."

It was like I was a teenager again. I nodded, reached over to grab the nearest chair, and pulled it up next to the bed. I sat there, back straight, as she studied me.

"What is your plan with Claire?" She folded her arms across her chest. She was trying to seem intimidating, but she just looked small in her hospital gown and big hospital bed. Her greying hair was pulled back into a bun, and she looked tired.

"Ms. Rose, I don't have any plans with Claire. She showed up at my house after some fight with her mom. She needed a place to stay while she looked for a more permanent situation." I raised my hands to show her that I had no ill will. The last thing on my mind was hurting Claire.

Rose's face dropped. "She had a fight with Ms. Hodges?"

I frowned. Was I not supposed to say something? Rose

and Claire were close. How did Rose not know? "Listen, I don't—"

"I should have figured that. As soon as I'm not around, Ms. Hodges can't let things lie. They were doing so well together." Rose dropped her gaze to her hands that were now fidgeting with the blanket draped across her lap.

I felt bad. I wished I could fix this, but I didn't know how. I knew that Claire had a rocky relationship with her mom. But beyond what little she told me that night she ripped my heart from my chest, I went out of my way to keep the Hodges family and their drama as far away from me as possible.

"Listen." Rose's hand was on mine, and her gaze was desperate. "Please, keep Claire safe. I have another day in here, but when I get out, I'll be around to fix what broke."

I could see the concern in her eyes, and her worry lines deepened as she stared up at me. There was only one other person in this world that cared about Claire as much as I did, and it was the woman sitting next to me. I wrapped my other hand around hers and patted it.

I offered her a calming smile as I said, "I promise you. I will not let anything bad happen to Claire. You have my word."

11

JUNIPER

SWEET TEA &
SOUTHERN GENTLEMAN

M y phone was ringing. Hot water pelted my back, but my shower was cut short from the shrill ring-tone coming from the other side of the curtain. I quickly rinsed out the conditioner that I had left in to saturate and flipped the water off.

I grabbed a towel and held it in front of my body as I stepped onto the bathmat and leaned forward to grab my phone. Just as I picked it up, the phone stopped ringing. I stared at the number. It was a local area code, and they didn't leave a message, which meant it was probably a tele-marketer.

"They work fast," I mumbled under my breath as I set my phone down and started to dry off.

I was annoyed that my shower had been cut short, but the mirror was completely fogged over, which told me I'd been in there for a while. It was probably time for me to get out.

After wrapping a towel around my body and another around my hair, I opened the bathroom door and stepped into my room. I dressed in a white shirt and jeans before heading back into the bathroom to dry my hair and put on a bit of makeup.

Dad really didn't talk to me after what happened yesterday with Kevin's mom. He just kept to himself, and Mom assigned me to the back, inventorying stock. When we got back to the house, Mom made dinner, and I fell asleep on the couch while they watched the news.

Mom woke me up before they went to bed and told me I'd get a crick in my neck if I spent the night on the couch. I groggily made my way to my room and fell asleep.

I felt better when I woke up this morning. I was ready to wash off the day before and start anew. After all, it was highly unlikely that Mrs. Proctor would come into Godwin's twice in one week. I was fairly certain that yesterday was an anomaly—a rare sighting that we wouldn't witness again for decades to come.

I just hoped Mom and Dad saw it the same way. The last thing I needed was for them to insist that I stay home because they were worried about me. Kevin had done that. He liked to control where I was and what I did. I was tired of it. I wanted my freedom.

I needed to feel useful, and working at the shop gave me

that. More than I realized before I'd agreed to help out there.

Once I had finished getting ready, I slipped my phone into my back pocket and headed out of my room and into the hallway. I didn't hear voices from the kitchen, but I could hear dishes being moved and water being run, so I knew my parents were in there.

I took a deep breath and rounded the corner. "Morning," I said in a chipper voice that sounded strange even to my ears.

Mom looked over her shoulder at me. She was in the process of washing a pan from last night's dinner. "Morning."

Dad was sitting at the table with a coffee cup in hand and a danish on a plate in front of him. He bought some food last night before we closed up and brought it home. He raised up his coffee mug in greeting.

I gave him an awkward smile and moved to join him at the table. The kitchen was quiet, and I didn't like it. It was almost as if I'd interrupted something. I glanced at Mom, who was now staring out the window as she washed the pan, and when I looked over at Dad, he was scrolling on his phone.

I left my phone on the table as I made my way toward the cereal cabinet for some breakfast. After my bowl was poured, I grabbed a spoon and went back to the table. I busied myself with eating. A few bites in, my phone rang again. It startled me and my parents. Everyone's gaze snapped to its location on the table.

I glanced down at the number, and it was the same one I'd missed earlier. I sighed and pressed on the side button to silence the ring.

"Who was it?" Mom asked.

I shrugged and took another bite of cereal. "I don't know. It's a local area code, but I don't recognize it. If they want me to call back, they can leave a message."

Mom nodded and turned her focus back to the dishes. My phone finally went dark when the call was finished. I returned to my cereal only to have my phone ring again.

It was the same number.

"Well, now you should answer it. It could be an emergency." Mom sounded exasperated, and I knew if this person kept calling, it would drive her nuts.

I raised my hands in surrender before I reached over and picked up my phone. I swallowed the bits of cereal in my mouth and pressed on the green button in the center of my screen.

"Hello?"

"So, you decided to finally answer my calls."

Kevin's familiar voice filled my ear, causing my entire body to go numb. My heart started to pound, and my breathing turned shallow as I stared at my phone. My mouth turned dry, and suddenly I couldn't swallow.

"I know you think you can run back to your parents and everything will be okay, but I miss you, baby. I promise, I didn't mean to hurt you. You just made me so mad when you accused me of cheating."

I tried to speak, but it was as if my vocal cords had been frozen. Nothing was going to get through.

"I know you still love me, and you didn't mean to leave." He sighed.

I hated that he sounded genuine. I hated that he knew the right words to say that would start reeling me back in. I wanted to be strong, but I felt so weak.

"Spend some time with your family, and then let's make a plan to meet up." He paused. "Can you do that?"

"Are you here?" I finally managed out.

I could hear his smile on the other side of the phone. "Of course, baby. I wasn't going to let you leave and not try to make things right. You want to see me, right?"

I wanted to say no. I wanted to tell him to go back. That we were finished. But right here, right now, wasn't the right time. I'd been with the man for so long, I'd forgotten who I was without him. The least I could do was tell him that we were finished to his face.

He deserved that.

"I'll see you," I whispered.

"Wonderful. How about tomorrow afternoon? Does that work?"

I swallowed, my mouth feeling like sandpaper. I nodded but then realized he couldn't see me, so I whispered, "Yes."

"I'll text you the address. Should we do noon?"

"Sure."

He told me he loved me and then said goodbye. He hung up, but I remained in my seat, frozen with my phone to my face. I closed my eyes, my stomach churning from the conversation we just had.

Kevin knew I was here, and he'd followed me. I was never going to get away from that man.

Suddenly, my stomach took a nosedive, and everything I'd just eaten for breakfast was making a quick reappearance. I pushed my chair away from the table, stumbled into the guest bathroom, and shut the door. I barely made it to the toilet before my stomach emptied and I was left shaking on the floor.

Once I was certain that I wasn't going to vomit again, I moved to rest my back against the tub, letting the chill of the porcelain seep through my shirt and cool my skin. I brought up my knees and rested my forehead on my hands. I took in methodical breaths with the hopes of calming my nerves.

Kevin found me, but that didn't mean I had to go back to him. He wanted to talk, and I knew I wasn't going to get closure if I kept my distance. So, I was going to go. We'd be in a public place. It wasn't like he would try anything when people could see.

I was going to be fine.

Three swift knocks followed by Mom's voice had me lifting my gaze toward the door. "Juniper? Are you okay?"

I nodded as I moved to place my hand on the ground and gingerly lift myself up to standing. "I'm fine," I said as I flushed the toilet and moved to the sink. "Just a little nauseous." I washed my hands and pulled the hand towel down to dry them.

Then I pulled open the door and startled when I saw just how close Mom was to me. She raked her gaze down my face before glancing around me.

"Are you sick?" she asked, lifting the back of her hand to my forehead.

I moved to dodge her, but she must have anticipated that because her hand moved with me. I paused and let her touch my forehead before I dipped down and slipped around her before she could stop me.

Now that I was out in the hallway, I threw up my hands as Mom whipped around, the look of fire in her gaze.

"I'm not five, and I'm fine. I get this way in the morning if I eat food too soon after I wake up." I waved toward my face. "I'm not sick..." I paused. "It's like I get motion sickness."

Mom folded her arms and narrowed her eyes. Realizing that she wasn't going to be appeased until she felt my skin for herself, I sighed and leaned forward. "Feel my head," I said.

She paused before she brought the back of her wrist to my forehead. She was studying the wall in front of her as if it held the answer to all of life's questions, but I knew she was just concentrating. Finally, she sighed and pulled her wrist back.

"You're not running a temperature." Then she leaned

closer to me. "Should I set you up a doctor's appointment? You should probably get looked at."

"I'm fine, Ma." I turned to make my way back toward the kitchen. "If I need to go to the doctor, I'll set up the appointment myself."

"It's really not a problem. I have Dr. Jacobs' number in my phone." She stayed a foot behind me as she followed me down the hall.

When we got back to the kitchen, she made a beeline for her phone. "I have it right here," she said as she held it up.

"Ma!" I wasn't in the mood for her to push me like this. My mind was still reeling from the call with Kevin. The last thing I needed was to try to navigate her insistence to take care of me.

"Leave her alone, Betty. She can take care of herself." Dad had set his phone down and was looking at Mom from over his readers.

I gave him a grateful smile before I picked up my half-eaten bowl of cereal and headed over to the sink. I rinsed the cereal and milk down the drain before pulling open the dishwasher to load my bowl and spoon.

"Was that Kevin?"

Ice rushed through my veins when I heard my ex's name on my dad's lips. I turned to see that he was now standing behind me, holding my phone. Mom was sputtering somewhere behind him, but I didn't search for her whereabouts. All I could think about was the look of pure anger on my father's face as he nodded toward my phone.

I didn't have to answer for Dad to know. His face fell as he placed my phone down on the counter. His movements were slow and meaningful. He was thinking before he spoke. It always seemed that the silence before he spoke was the most deafening.

"I'm not going to assume that I know what's going on between you and Kevin," he finally said as he turned around to face me.

I don't know why I thought he would be angry, but when his gaze met mine, he looked sad. And it broke my heart. The last thing I wanted to do was dump my problems at my parents' feet. I should be able to handle my life and my relationships without dragging them into it.

I should be a better daughter.

"I'm sorry, Dad," I whispered.

He waved away my words. "It is my job to protect you, and I did a bad job of that."

I stepped forward, ready to rebut his words, but he just held up his hand to silence me.

"That is the job of every father. To protect his daughter."

Realizing that if I spoke, I was only going to upset him, I moved until I was leaning against the counter and gave him my full attention.

"I'm not going to stop you from seeing Kevin. If you love him and you want to be with him, your mother and I will do what we need to to support you." His voice cracked from emotion, and suddenly the tears I'd been trying to keep at bay filled my eyes and threatened to spill.

"I know you will," I whispered.

Mom had moved to stand next to Dad. She didn't look as supportive as he did, but I knew she cared. I knew that she hated Kevin and the last thing she wanted was for me to go back to him. But if that was my choice, I knew she would support me.

"We're just getting together for lunch tomorrow. That's it."

"He's here in Harmony?" Mom's face turned red, but after one look from Dad, she took in a deep breath and pinched her lips.

"Will you do something for your father?" he asked.

I studied him, not quite sure what he had in mind. But he looked so earnest, I just nodded. "Okay," I said slowly. "What did you have in mind?"

12

CLAIRE

SWEET TEA & SOUTHERN GENTLEMAN

"Claire."

I moaned and shifted my head that was resting in the crook of my arm. "Just one more minute."

"Claire!" Rose's voice was harsher and more determined.

I reluctantly opened my eyes and sat up. I'd been napping on the edge of her bed, and I was irritated to be woken up like this. I wiped at the corners of my mouth and glared at her.

"Why did you wake me up?" I asked as I pulled at the corners of the blanket one of the nurses had been so kind to get for me. I sunk into the chair back.

Rose raised her forefinger to her lips. "I think I hear your mother's voice."

My body went cold. I stilled everything but my pounding heart and tipped my ear toward the door to listen.

I'd been here all morning and afternoon. Abigail was going to pick me up in about ten minutes. Rose and I ate lunch together, watched a few of her favorite movies, and laughed. She finally got out of me what happened with Mom. And while she didn't say too much, she patted my hand and told me that my mom still cared even if she had a strange way of showing it.

Rose took a nap, and apparently, so did I. Which I was now regretting as I desperately tried to wipe the cobwebs of sleep from my brain. If Rose was, in fact, correct, and my mother was moments away from walking into this room, I couldn't afford to be groggy.

"Maybe I should go to the bathroom," I muttered as I quickly stood and turned to make a beeline for the open door.

"Claire, wait," Rose said as she reached out and grabbed my hand.

I wanted to pull away. My body was in self-preservation mode, and my fight or flight was kicking in. The last thing I wanted to do was fight Rose, so I took in a deep breath and looked at her.

"The first step in healing is to face the challenge head-on. Avoidance will do you no good." Her expression was genuine, and she had just gone through surgery, so the least I could do was appease her.

I narrowed my eyes and jutted my free forefinger at her. I wanted to leave, but I would stay for her. "You aren't being fair, you know this."

She chuckled as she patted my hand with her other one. I reached behind me and pulled the chair forward before I sat.

"That's why you love me," she said.

I loved that she looked so genuinely happy that I was going to remain in the room, even though it was the last thing I wanted to do. I liked making Rose happy. I just wished her happiness wasn't tied to me talking to my mother.

I held my breath as I listened to the voices and sounds coming from the hallway. I was chanting, *It's going to be okay*, over and over in my mind, but it wasn't making me feel any better. I wished I had a place to hide. A place where I felt safe.

I was living with Jax. The one guy my mother would kill if she found out I was there. Panic filled my chest as I leaned in toward Rose.

"Don't tell her that I'm staying at Jax's house," I whispered.

Rose patted my hand. "Mum's the word."

Seconds felt like hours, and just as Rose had predicted, my mother walked through the door. She was using a cane, but that woman was as stubborn as she was critical. There was no way she was going to let her hip surgery keep her down. She was up and insisting that she could do it on her own as soon as the hospital let her out.

The way my mother's expression fell when she saw me sitting next to Rose, told me all I needed to know about where I stood with her. Her frown deepened, and her eyes narrowed as she looked me over, before settling her gaze on my hand which was still clutching Rose's.

"Claire," she said, in a way that she would speak of a bug who just hit her windshield. "I didn't know you were here. Or that you were still in town." She cleared her throat and then adjusted her weight so both of her hands could rest on her cane.

I knew what she was doing. She wanted me to know that she was in charge. That she was the boss. Her body always spoke louder than her words. I shot Rose an *I told you so* look and hurried out of my chair.

"I was just leaving," I said as I glanced down at my watch. Even if Abigail wasn't going to be here for another five minutes, waiting out front for her trumped sitting in this room in awkward silence with my mother.

Before Rose could speak—and I could see that she was about to—I waved goodbye to both of them and bolted out the door. I didn't stop until I felt the sun on my face and the fresh outside air filled my lungs. I tucked myself into a corner near the front of the building in case my mother tried to follow me—but I doubted she would.

Thankfully, my phone chimed a few minutes later. It was a text from Abigail saying that she was here. I hurried out of my hiding spot and pulled open her door. She startled, reaching her hand into her purse as if she thought I was going to rob her.

I plopped down on the seat and slammed the door. I

turned to her and gave her a wide smile. "Hey." Then my gaze dropped to her hand still stuck in her purse. "Whatcha doing?"

Abigail's panicked expression finally morphed into one of calm as she laughed and pulled a black bottle from her purse. "I was literally about to pepper spray you."

I glanced at the bottle and then back to her. "Well, thank you for not doing that."

"I thought it was going to take you a minute to get out here." She dropped the bottle back into her purse and then set her purse down next to me. "You had me thinking someone was going to steal my car."

I shook my head. "Nope. Just ready to get out of here."

Abigail nodded as she put her car into drive, and I buckled my seatbelt. We kept the conversation light as she drove to her apartment. I'd never been to her place, but it sounded like heaven compared to Jax's house. I was ready to spend some time with other girls and just unwind.

"You got booze, right?" I asked as she pulled in behind her building and parked her car.

"Of course. I've got lots of booze."

I grinned at her. "Awesome."

I followed her up the back stairs and down the hallway to her apartment. Music could be heard from inside as she unlocked the door. The lights were dimmed, and just as we passed by the kitchen, I caught sight of a plethora of food.

Two women were standing in the living room. One was older and holding a baby. The other one was younger with her dark hair pulled up into a ponytail. She looked like Abigail's identical twin.

"Claire, come meet my sister, Sabrina, and my dad's wife, Penny."

I walked over to join Abigail. Both women turned to look at me. They smiled and shook my hand. Sabrina introduced me to her son, Samuel, before Penny stretched out her hands and insisted that it was time she left the girls to their night. She cooed and cuddled Samuel as she disappeared down the hallway.

I looked back at Sabrina, who looked a bit weary, but when she noticed me watching her, she smiled. "So did you grow up here?" Sabrina asked when Abigail excused herself to answer the door.

I nodded. "Yeah. My mom runs Apple Blossom B&B."

"Ah, Missy?"

I really didn't want to talk about my mom, so I cursed myself for bringing her up. "Yep."

Sabrina gave me a knowing look, but before she could say anything, the room began to fill with people. Abigail returned with Shelby, my brother's ex-girlfriend, and two other women I'd never seen before.

My heart stopped when Shelby's gaze met mine. I was a few years younger than Clint, so I was never really involved in his drama. I just knew he blew off Shelby, broke her heart, and she left town. I didn't know she was back, and I feared what she would say when she saw me.

Shelby studied me for a moment before she crossed the

room. I braced myself when she got over to me, and when she raised her hands, I thought this was the end. She was going to hit me. But suddenly, her arms wrapped around me, and she pulled me close.

"Claire," she said as she squeezed me tight. "It's been so long."

"You know each other?" Abigail suddenly appeared next to us, holding two fruity alcoholic drinks.

Shelby pulled back. "I dated her brother, remember?"

Abigail took a sip before handing me the other drink. "That's right."

"Claire was the sweetest of that family." Shelby smiled at me. "I'm glad you're here."

This was not the encounter that I'd expected today, but it was turning out to be a good one. Clint was a jerk, which was why I never spoke to him. I didn't know the details of what he'd done to Shelby, but I never believed any of the things he said. He always made a point of telling a story the way that painted him in the best light.

I never trusted him.

"Have you met Tamara or Ella?" Shelby asked as she stepped to the side, and the two women she came in with moved to stand next to her.

I shook my head. "I haven't."

"Tamara is Belle's mom. She's back in town after leaving a few years ago."

"Belle?"

Shelby smiled. "She's my step-daughter. I just married

Miles." She lifted her left hand and wiggled her fingers, her diamond glittering in the light.

I raised my eyebrows. "Miles? As in Clint's best friend and your ex-stepbrother?"

Shelby nodded. "It's a long story. We'll have to get lunch sometime, so we can catch up. You know, since we're the ones who grew up in Harmony."

"I'd like that. Although, I don't know how long I'll be staying."

"Your mom?"

I faked a gasp before I nodded. "How did you know?"

She just chuckled. "Lucky guess, I suppose."

I glanced over to the other woman next to her. She had long brown hair and glasses. She smiled and reached out her hand. "I'm Ella."

"Right, sorry. This is Ella. She's from Pennsylvania. She moved here to write for the Harmony Island Gazette. The inn was her first piece, that's how we met."

"Oh, cool." I shook her hand. "I'm Claire. My family runs the Apple Blossom B&B."

Recognition passed through Ella's gaze. "Your mom is Missy?"

I nodded. "Yep."

"I've met her. She marched right into my office the day the piece about the inn came out and demanded that I do the same for the B&B."

"Ha! That sounds like my mom." This is why I stayed away. I could never just be Claire. I was always, Claire, daughter of the town's crazy person. It had been hard when I was a kid, and after being here for a month, it was clear nothing had changed. It was just as hard.

I was tired of living under her shadow.

"Should we drink?" I asked, lifting the glass Abigail had handed me.

Abigail whooped as she lifted her hands in the air. Sabrina pressed play, and soon the apartment was filled with music. We ate and drank. It was amazing just to hang out with a group of women. We laughed and played beer pong. The neighbors only came once to ask us to turn the music down, which we did.

We were all pretty buzzed, except for Juniper, who said that she had some important meeting tomorrow that she couldn't be hungover for. Which had me thinking maybe I should be a bit more careful as well. But then memories of Mom or Jax would flood my mind, and I would pour myself another lime margarita that Abigail had whipped up.

Sabrina excused herself to go to bed. I guess Samuel was an early riser. Tamara, Shelby, and Ella left as soon as Miles came to pick them up. He waved at me, and I waved back. I'd thought he was the most handsome guy in Harmony High when he was best friends with my brother. And even years later, nothing much had changed.

Thankfully, I was lying on the couch next to Abigail, so all of my thoughts stayed in my head instead of slipping through my loose, drunk lips and making Miles feel awkward. Juniper left soon after, leaving Abigail and me alone.

She looked over at me before she patted me on the leg. "Well, I think the night's over." She started to stand, but I just groaned and grabbed onto her hand.

"No. Let's watch a movie." I let go of her hand so I could entwine my fingers together in a begging manner.

She eyed me. "Bash is going to be here in the morning. He couldn't get away from work earlier this week, and I want to be rested for when he gets here." She stretched her arms above her head and yawned.

I felt like a bad friend, but I couldn't go back to Jax's house. Not right now. I just needed a little more time away from my sucky life.

"I just...don't want to be alone right now," I whined. I sounded small and pathetic, but it was true. "But if you really want me to go, I'll go." I grabbed my phone from my back pocket. "I'll request a ride right now." I swiped at my screen, and it illuminated me. I clicked on the ride share app, but before I could do anything, she pulled the phone from my hand.

"No, no. Don't do that. We can just hang out here." She smiled over at me. "A movie sounds great."

We spent the next two hours watching a chick flick from our childhood. I opened a bottle of wine and offered it to Abigail, but she just raised her hand and shook her head, so I drank alone.

I wasn't really sure what happened after the movie. My

head was cloudy, and I couldn't really think straight. I knew I was in the car with Abigail, and she said something about getting me some food or I was going to be miserable tomorrow.

Suddenly, I was lifted off her couch by people on either side of me, and from the soft, feminine voice beside me, I figured it was someone Abigail knew. She told me her name was Penny, but my mind was so cluttered, I didn't remember who that was.

After they forced me to eat a hamburger, they drove me back to Jax's house. I couldn't walk straight, so I leaned most of my weight on their shoulders as they walked me to Jax's front door.

Thankfully, the door was unlocked, so they helped me in, and I veered toward the couch. Walking to my bed sounded like more work than I wanted to do right now. Abigail and Penny protested, but I dropped down on the cushions before they could stop me.

I grabbed a nearby pillow and hugged it to my chest. "So soft," I whispered as I began to pet it.

"Should we stay here?" Abigail asked.

Penny's response was muffled, and it would take too much work to try to focus my attention long enough to pick up on what she was saying.

"I'll call Jax."

"Jax," I murmured as I tipped to the side. My entire body suddenly felt way too heavy. I just needed to lie down to feel better.

"Hey, I'm dropping Claire off at your house, but she's a little drunk. I'm worried about her being here alone."

Silence. I cracked one eye open to see if they had left, but Abigail was still standing there with the phone pressed to her head.

"Oh, if you can do that, that would be great." She paused. "You'll be here in ten minutes?" Silence. "If you think that's okay, we'll head back."

I don't remember Abigail leaving. All I remembered was her shaking my shoulder and telling me something. What that something was, I had no idea. I just closed my eyes and nodded, hoping that would get her to stop talking to me. My head hurt, and I wanted to stop thinking and go to sleep.

My entire body was relaxed, and I could feel myself drifting in and out of consciousness, when suddenly, two hands gripped my shoulders, and I was pulled into a sitting position. My body went into fight mode. I ripped my eyes open, and my fists went flying.

"Whoa, whoa!" Jax's voice filled the air as his hands dropped to grab my fists. "What are you doing? Claire, it's me."

My entire body sank into the couch as I squinted at him. "Jax?"

He dropped down so that he was at eye level with me. "Who did you think it was?"

I shrugged, my head pounding from the sudden movements I was making. "A kidnapper."

He snorted. "Who would kidnap you? Especially in this

condition." He grabbed my hand. "Come on, let's get you up and in your bed." He stood and pulled on my hand as if that was all it was going to take to get me moving.

"Why are you here? I thought you were working." I was comfortable. I didn't want to move.

"Abigail called me. Told me that you were a mess. Remus is watching the pub while I came home to take care of you."

I wrinkled my nose. "Remus. Bleh."

"What's wrong with Remus?" He must have realized that I was not in the mood to move because he just dropped my hand and pinched the bridge of his nose like this conversation was going to be the death of him.

"He doesn't like me." I raised my forefinger in his direction. It swayed no matter how hard I tried to keep it steady. "He told me that I should stay away from you. That I broke your heart."

Jax just stared at me. "He said that, did he?"

"Ha!" I said. It must have come out loud because Jax raised his eyebrows. "I broke your heart. *You* broke *my* heart." I glared at him.

He studied me before he pushed his hand through his hair and glanced around. "I really don't want to get into this while you're drunk. Will you just come with me? You'll feel better once you sleep the alcohol off."

"You just want to get rid of me," I said, my words slurring even though I was desperately trying to keep my composure.

"I don't want to get rid of you." He bent down, resting his hands on either side of my legs and stared at me. "I just want to help you to your room."

I narrowed my eyes at him. "You never wanted me here. My life. My family. Us. It was too complicated. We were never going to work."

He stared at me. I couldn't read his expression, but that might have been because he seemed to be swaying ever so slightly.

"What do you want from me, Claire?"

I studied his face. His familiar eyes. Even though we were both older, he still looked like the boy I walked away from years ago. Why wouldn't he just admit that our relationship had been a lie? Just a ruse to torture my family once more.

My gaze drifted down his nose to his lips. I knew what they felt like pressed to mine. I knew what it was like to kiss Jax. I wondered if it felt the same. Had he changed so much that his kisses had changed too?

Suddenly, all the reasons I hated him left my mind, and all I wanted to do was kiss him. To prove to myself that the memories I kept locked away in the Pandora's box of my mind weren't as good as I remembered them to be.

"Sit next to me," I whispered.

He raised his eyebrows. "Then you'll come with me to your room?"

I nodded.

He sighed before he turned and dropped down next to me. "Happy?"

All inhibition left my mind as I shifted my weight and straddled him on the couch. My thighs burned from the heat of his legs. I sank down into his lap and held his gaze.

I must have shocked him. He pulled his body back, but I wasn't going to let him go. I caged him in between my arms as I rested my hands on either side of his head. My hair cascaded down on one side, creating a curtain.

"What are you doing?" he asked.

I held his gaze before I glanced down at his lips. "Do you think our kisses feel the same?"

His expression stilled as he stared at me. "What?"

"My lips. Do you think they feel the same?" I lifted one of my hands so I could gently run my fingers across his lips. "I'm wondering if yours feel like they did before." I glanced back up at him. There was a fire in his gaze that ignited an inferno in my gut.

"Kiss me," I whispered.

Jax just stared at me. "What?"

"Kiss me," I said again, this time more demanding.

His hands that were resting on the couch suddenly grabbed my upper thighs as he pulled my body to his. He pulled his head off the couch, his lips inches away from mine.

"You want me to kiss you, Claire?" His voice was deep and daring.

I wasn't thinking. No warning bells were going off in my mind. All I wanted was his lips on mine.

"Yes."

One of his hands released my thigh and he buried his fingers in my hair. He pulled me to him, my lips crashing into his. It startled me at first, but I got over the shock as my hands cradled his face and our lips moved in sync with each other.

I slid even closer to him, my body pressed to every part of his. He groaned against my mouth as his hand moved from my thigh to cup my rear end. I pushed myself up onto my knees and Jax followed me.

He parted my lips with his tongue, and I let him in. My hair fell like a curtain around us, heightening the heat and passion flowing between our bodies like electricity.

His arm wrapped around my waist and he pulled me to the side, laying me down on the couch with his body pressed into mine. The heat between us was a fire I would never be able to put out.

When he broke our kiss, I whimpered, not wanting it to end. He had both hands on either side of my head, holding his body up so he could stare down at me. There was something in his gaze, something that I couldn't read but I somehow understood.

I knew because I felt the same.

My fingers found the hem of his shirt before finding his warm skin. My hands danced around his abs, then his chest, lifting his shirt higher and higher as I went. Jax studied me. I could see hesitation in his gaze, but I wasn't going to stop.

Not now.

Suddenly, Jax shifted his weight to one arm while he used his other hand to pull his shirt the rest of the way off. I stared at his bare chest in front of me. My fingers touching, feeling every part of him. This was new. This was different.

Then, in the moonlight, I saw the necklace. It hung down from his neck. My fingers found the chain and I slid them down until I got to the ring at the bottom. A ring I'd never seen before.

It was a woman's ring.

That Jax was wearing.

Around his neck.

My stomach plummeted, and suddenly, I wanted to throw up. Here, I thought that Jax and I had a similar experience. I thought he'd never moved on, because there was no way I could move on.

Not with someone different. Not with someone who wasn't Jax.

But no, he had moved on. And wherever that woman was, he still wanted her. That's why her ring was around his neck.

My stomach lurched, and I wished I hadn't drunk so much. I pushed and wiggled to get Jax off of me. If he didn't move fast, I was going to vomit on him and his couch.

"Claire, wha—" One look at me and Jax stood. He

helped me up, but I just shoved him away as I ran to the bathroom.

I slammed the door on his startled face, lifted the toilet seat, and spilled the contents of my stomach. I wanted to believe that the tears streaming down my cheeks were from the force in which my muscles were expelling the alcohol in my body, but that would be a lie.

Those were the tears of a broken heart.

When I was finally finished, I collapsed against the tub and closed my eyes. I was exhausted. My body had gone on an emotional roller coaster, and I was fairly certain I couldn't move, even if I wanted to.

I wasn't sure how long I was in the bathroom for, but after a few soft knocks, I heard the door open and Jax call my name.

I wasn't ready to face him or what we'd done, so I just remained still with my eyes closed, hoping he'd just leave me to sleep on the bathroom floor.

I felt two hands slide under my back and knees as he hoisted me up and pulled me against his chest. My head rested on his shoulder as he carried me from the bathroom and into my room. He gently laid me down on the bed before taking off my shoes and covering me with a blanket. He left only to return a minute later with a glass of water and some pain meds that he left on the nightstand next to me.

I heard him leave my room for the final time, and I

curled up into a ball, hugging the pillows around me and softly crying into them.

I thought my heart had broken the night I didn't go meet him. I thought I'd experienced pain when I looked into his eyes and told him that we were finished. I was wrong.

This was pain.

And I was going to be forever broken.

13

JAX

SWEET TEA & SOUTHERN GENTLEMAN

D ammit.

It was seven in the morning, and I hadn't slept a wink. After I finally got Claire to bed, I left some water and pain meds on her nightstand and headed back out to the pub. Remus could tell that there was something wrong with me, but I didn't want to talk. I kept to myself as we filled the final drink orders and shut the pub down for the night.

He clapped me on the back before he left and wished me good luck—he didn't say with what, but I knew he understood that the reason for my struggle was Claire. I didn't confirm it, but there was a silent understanding between us.

When I got home, I checked on Claire. She was out cold. I studied her for a moment before I felt like a creeper and shut her door.

The kiss we shared had felt like a dream, and there were

moments where I asked myself if I had really kissed her, or if my imagination had run wild. I wanted to believe that it was true as badly as I wanted to believe I'd made the whole thing up.

Dreaming that I'd kissed her was a reality I was comfortable with. Actually kissing her was a nightmare that I feared I would never wake up from if it were real.

I'd kissed Claire...and I wanted to do it again.

I ripped off my covers and got out of bed. There was no use trying to sleep. Claire was haunting every part of my life. At least when I was awake, I could push those thoughts to a dark corner of my mind. One where I refused to go.

When I was asleep, my mind liked to torture me with dreams that made me wake up confused and frustrated.

I stomped into the bathroom, where I flipped on the shower. I was just going to have to go without sleep while Claire was here. That was all.

I showered, wrapped a towel around my waist, and stepped out onto the plush bathmat that Remus had told me would change my life—he was right. After I dressed, I towel-dried my hair while watching a video on my phone. When I was finished, I'd successfully only thought about Claire once or twice, so I felt composed enough to leave my room.

I headed down the hallway and into the kitchen, where I breathed a sigh of relief. I was alone. I wasn't sure where Gramps was. He liked to sleep in some days, and on others, he was up before the sun had hit the horizon.

I opened the fridge and grabbed the gallon of milk.

Today felt like a cereal type of day. When I headed over to the cupboard where the bowls were, my gaze drifted to the window outside, and my whole body stopped. Claire was crouched down in the middle of my yard, scratching Carmel's ears. She looked a little worse for wear, but with how drunk she was last night, I was impressed she was up and moving.

I hated that she was wearing shorts and a white tank. Her skin glowed in the early morning light, and her hair was illuminated in a way that had me wondering if it felt as soft as it looked.

I ripped my gaze from her and growled to myself, "Get your head on straight, man."

Thinking about Claire in any other way than as my ex was going to get me in trouble.

"She probably doesn't even remember what happened last night," I murmured to myself as I grabbed a bowl from the shelf and set it down on the counter in front of me. "You're the idiot that can't let go. Don't make stupid decisions."

I turned to head to the pantry when Gramps came into view. I yelped and jumped back, grateful that I didn't have anything in my hands because I would have hurled it at him. His eyebrows went up. He must have sensed that I was on edge.

"Morning," I said, trying to redeem myself. I gave him a grin that probably did nothing to convince him that I was completely rational and in control of my life.

Gramps stared at me. "What happened last night?"

My entire body flushed as I sidestepped Gramps and headed to the pantry for some cereal. "What do you mean?" Had he seen me and Claire making out on the couch? Or had he just overheard me talking to myself?

I inwardly groaned. I should have never let Claire back into my life. She was complication personified. Remus was right. She would do nothing for me but mess with my head.

"Just now, you said, 'She probably doesn't even remember what happened last night.' "

He did a spot-on impression of me, and if I wasn't so disoriented, I would have complimented him. "Claire was drunk last night and threw up. I was just wondering if she remembered."

Gramps narrowed his eyes as he stared at me. I could tell that he didn't believe me, but I didn't care. I didn't understand my feelings, and I knew talking about them would only confuse me more. No. They belonged in the lockbox of my mind where no one could be a witness to them.

Thankfully, Gramps filled his mug with coffee and shuffled back to his room. I waited for the sound of his door shutting before I let out the breath I'd been holding. I grabbed the box of cereal and returned to where I'd left my bowl and filled it. I poured the milk, grabbed a spoon, and took a bite. Just as I started chewing, the back door opened. I didn't have to look to know who had just come in.

I closed my eyes for a second to prepare myself before I turned around, still holding my bowl of cereal and spoon.

Claire's eyes were wide as she stood just inside of the kitchen with the door still open behind her. I forced myself to be calm as I nodded to her in acknowledgement.

"Morning," she whispered as she moved to slip off her shoes and shut the door behind her.

How was she this awake? She had been drunk last night. That was the only explanation for why she told me to kiss her and then threw up. She was an anomaly with the way she was holding her composure.

"Hey," was all I could manage to say around the cereal and the milk.

She pinched her lips together and nodded as she stepped further into the kitchen. I didn't drop my gaze right away. Instead, I just studied her. She looked tired. It made me wonder if she was really okay or if she was just pretending to be.

She moved toward me, and out of instinct, I stepped away. She gave me a small smile as she murmured, "Cereal sounds good."

I nodded as I took another bite.

She grabbed a bowl and filled it with the cereal I'd left on the counter.

"I'm surprised," I said after I swallowed a bite.

She glanced over her shoulder at me while she gingerly poured the milk. "Surprised by what?"

I shrugged and nodded toward her full bowl. "I figured you'd want something a bit heartier to counteract the alcohol. Like eggs and bacon."

Claire's face flushed as she nodded. "I ate some earlier. I woke up with the worst stomachache." She sighed as she grabbed her bowl and spoon and leaned against the counter to eat.

The silence that fell between us was deafening. I wanted to ask her if she remembered what happened last night. She looked so calm and relaxed. While I felt like a mess. Did she not care? Was this a game? I was certain I was going to go crazy if she didn't start talking and soon.

She took another bite, and just when I thought I was going insane, she met my gaze. "Did you help me get to bed last night?"

And with that one sentence, my heart plummeted through my body, down through the floor of the house, and buried itself six feet under the ground. I stopped chewing and stared at her. She blinked a few times like my reaction had startled her.

Get it together, flashed through my mind in bright red blinking letters. I forced a cough and slowly chewed the cereal before swallowing. "Um, yeah. I did." I shrugged like it hadn't been a big deal. "Abigail and Penny drove you back, and I took over from there."

Claire studied me for a moment before she nodded. But then she frowned as she glanced around before her gaze landed back on me. "But didn't you have to work last night?"

I'd already put another bite of cereal in my mouth, so I quickly said, "She called me to see if I'd come help you get into bed." I tipped my head back so the food wouldn't spill out.

"Oh."

We ate in silence for a few more bites. My stomach was in knots, and I wasn't enjoying the cereal or this conversation. All I wanted to do was grab my fishing gear and get out of this house and away from Claire.

I crossed the room and dumped my cereal out into the sink. I thought that Claire would move because she was now just a foot away from me. But she didn't. Instead, she watched me.

Anger boiled up. Did she really not remember that we kissed last night? Or was it so unimportant that she didn't want to bring it up? Did she think it was a mistake? Did she not feel what I felt last night when she climbed up onto my lap?

Every part of my body had responded to her. She was exactly how I remembered, and yet, there was something new about her that had me yearning to find out more. She was the perfect puzzle piece for me, but this time we were doing a different puzzle. I wasn't sure what the picture would turn out to be, but there was nothing I wanted more than to see it.

With my bowl and spoon now rinsed, I turned to face her, parting my lips but not knowing exactly what I wanted to say. Her eyes widened, and a flash of concern passed over her face.

"I'm going out with Brett today," she blurted out before I could speak.

I stopped, my lips parted, but all ability to speak instantly left my body. This was her answer to my question. The one I wanted to ask her but didn't know how.

And now I didn't have to.

"He said that there are some apartments opening up in his friend's building. I told him that my stay here is temporary, so I asked him if he knew of any place that would do a short-term lease that I could afford." She offered me a small smile like that was going to make me feel better.

"And they allow dogs?" I asked, motioning toward Carmel who was now lying out on the deck in the sun.

Claire flicked her gaze over to the window and then back to me. "Well...no."

I scoffed. This was typical Claire. Making decisions for everyone else. Walking away from everyone who cared about her—depended on her. I should have known she would never change.

"So, what's your plan?"

She was finished with her cereal now. The bowl was on the counter with just milk remaining. Claire slipped her hands into the front pockets of her shorts and glanced around. "I guess I was hoping to see if she could stay..." I raised my eyebrows. "With Brett. I'm sure he's okay with that."

I clenched my jaw at the mention of Brett. "No."

Claire looked surprised. "No?"

I stepped away from the sink before pushing my hands through my hair. "I told you that I would take responsibility for Carmel. I'm going to help. She can stay with me."

"I'm not holding you responsible for the situation she's in. You didn't know." She gave me a smile, but it just made me madder. "How could you have known?" She took a step closer to me with her hand extended. "I've put you out long enough. Once I get a place and things calm down, maybe we can be friends again."

My mouth tasted sour. Somehow, she was breaking up with me—and I hadn't even started dating the damn woman again.

I wasn't going to stand here and beg her not to go. If she wanted to leave, I was going to let her.

"Whatever you want, Claire. You can take her, 'cause you're right. This arrangement was temporary." I forced a smile as I stared down at her. "You're free to go whenever you want."

She studied me for what felt like an eternity, even though I was sure it was only a few seconds. I wasn't going to be the one to break the stare, so I held it, willing her to say something about the kiss last night.

She had felt something. I knew in my gut she felt what I did. She was just stubborn and scared.

"Thank you," she whispered as she dropped her gaze and stepped back. "I appreciate your help, but it's time for me to find my own place."

"Great." I gave her a grin that felt like the largest lie I'd ever told. I walked over to the back door and grabbed my boots. I shoved my feet into them, and from the corner of my eye I could see Claire hadn't moved. Instead, she was standing there, watching me.

"I'm going to go do some fishing," I said as I wrapped my hand around the door handle and pulled the door open.

"Oh."

I glanced back at Claire, who had her arms wrapped around her chest as if she were giving herself a hug. She met my gaze again, and there was something in it that I couldn't quite read, but I knew I didn't want to know.

"I'm going to jump in the shower, then. Brett should be here soon to get me."

My smile felt like a jack-o'-lantern's. "Great. I'll see you later."

I didn't wait for her to speak as I stepped out onto the deck and pulled the door shut behind me. I didn't stop moving as I crossed the porch and headed across the yard to my shed. After gathering my fishing supplies, I shut the door and walked around to my truck.

I tossed the items into the back, and the sound of them bouncing around the bed of the truck filled the quiet morning air. I climbed into my truck and started the engine. I glanced over at the front window to see that the kitchen was now empty. Claire was gone.

I cursed under my breath as I put my truck into reverse and peeled out of my driveway. I rolled my window down, resting my arm on the door to let the cool breeze wash over my skin. I was ready to get that woman out of my head.

I was ready to forget.

A fishing trip wasn't the healing balm I needed, but, for now, it would do.

14

JUNIPER

SWEET TEA & SOUTHERN GENTLEMAN

The store was dark when Dad pulled open the back door. He stepped to the side while he held the door open. The early morning light spilled into the dark hallway, illuminating the floor as I walked inside. I glanced over my shoulder to see Dad still standing there, watching Mom grab some papers from the car. Not wanting to give my parents an opening to ask me about the lunch plans I had with Kevin today, I disappeared further inside.

Last night, I'd spent the evening at Abigail's, and when I got home, Mom and Dad were asleep. I lingered in my room this morning until the last possible moment, and when I did leave, I hurried past them to get to the car. My stomach was rumbling—I was starving—but I wanted to avoid their questions more than I wanted to eat.

Plus, they literally owned a grocery store. Food was

everywhere. I just needed a minute to slip away and buy a doughnut from the bakery.

Whatever Dad had planned for me, he hadn't said. After our conversation yesterday, Dad just said he had some thoughts he needed to work out in his mind, and that he would let me know once he knew more.

It sounded cryptic and ominous, and I was really dreading our next conversation. I'd promised that I would listen to his suggestions and give them some thought before I wrote them off. I loved my parents, but this was my life. I was strong enough to stay away from Kevin if I wanted to.

And right now, I wanted to stay far, far away from him. But we had a history. He deserved to have me hear him out. It was the least I could do.

I lingered outside of Mom's office until I heard the low hum of my parents' voices as they joined me. I took a few steps down the hallway. Mom and Dad were deep in conversation as Mom neared her office door and pulled out her keys.

She glanced over at me once before turning her attention to the door and unlocking it. I slowly let out my breath as she walked into her office. I just might get through the day without having to address the giant elephant in the room. I had a small glimmer of hope that my parents forgot about my lunch plans and I was going to avoid a conversation about it.

I took a step closer to her now open office door, hoping

they would just give me my assignment and send me on my way.

"Juniper?" Mom called out to me.

Just the assignment. Please. Just the assignment. I chanted in my mind as I stepped into the doorway. "Yeah?"

She was sitting at her desk and reading a piece of paper. "Can you tidy up the stockroom? Dad hired a new guy, and he'll be here later. I'll have you training him on stocking the shelves, but the stockroom is a mess." She glanced over at me from above her paper. "Let's make a good first impression, shall we?"

She held my gaze. I paused, waiting for there to be more, but it never came. Instead, her eyebrows went up as if to accentuate her question, so I quickly nodded. "For sure." I hurried from her office before she could say anything further. Cleaning the stockroom, I could do. That was easy.

When I got to the stockroom, boxes were scattered around on the floor, and packing material had been left inside of them. I grabbed my earbuds from my purse and slipped them into my ears. I turned on my favorite oldies channel and started to clean up.

I grabbed a large black trash bag and began to fill it with the packing material from the boxes. Once I had three trash bags bursting with garbage, I tied them up, grabbed the knots and dragged the bags to the back door. I used my hip to push on the door release and walked out to the parking lot.

I sang along with the music as I pushed open the black

lid that closed over the dumpster and let it bang against the back. Then I heaved the first bag inside. The second went in as well. Just as I reached over to grab the last bag, my fingers brushed a hand that was not mine.

I yelped and turned to see a man standing there, holding the garbage bag. He had on a black hoodie and a pair of jeans. He stared down at me as my fight-or-flight instincts kicked in. Before I could process what I was doing, I balled my hand into a fist, punched him in the gut, and took off running.

I didn't stop until I was through the back door and ran into Mom's office. I must have looked like a wild woman because her expression was one of shock and confusion. I pulled out my earbuds before I doubled over. I took in deep breaths as the adrenaline mixed with the physical exertion caught up with me.

"Man..." I wheezed. "Garbage..." I took in a few more breaths.

"What?" Mom asked, not even trying to decipher my words.

I pinched my lips shut as I took in some calming breaths and my pounding heart calmed. "There was a man outside at the dumpster. He stole my garbage bag."

Mom looked more confused than ever. "What?"

Dad had come in now and was glancing from me to Mom. "What happened?"

"Juniper said some man was trying to steal our garbage."

Dad frowned. "Our garbage?"

I nodded and waved toward the back door. "I punched him and ran."

Dad kept his gaze on me as he headed out into the hallway and then disappeared from sight. I walked over to one of the chairs in Mom's office and collapsed on it. My stomach was churning as if it were trying to digest everything that had just happened.

The sound of deep voices grew louder. I peered at Mom's open door, trying to figure out why Dad had invited this man into the store. My suspicions were confirmed when Dad appeared in the doorway with a very confused-looking man.

If he hadn't freaked me out earlier, I would have allowed myself to notice he was attractive. His dark hair was tousled, and I hadn't noticed his bright blue eyes before. His gaze darted to me and then back to Mom. He pulled up the sleeves of his hoodie, revealing that he was muscular. My punch had to have been just a tap to him.

Suddenly, I felt like an idiot. What was I thinking? Obviously, I hadn't been thinking, or I wouldn't have embarrassed myself like that.

"This is Boone," Dad said as he waved his hand to garbage man before he glanced pointedly over at me. "He's the new hire."

Heat rushed through my entire body, and my mouth dropped open, but no words came out. My gaze snapped to Boone, but he was just standing there silently. Maybe he was just as embarrassed as I was. After all, what kind of person just sneaks up on someone like that?

If he had just kept his distance, our meeting could have been normal, and I wouldn't have felt as stupid as I did right then. I wouldn't be red hot from embarrassment.

Mom and Dad were glancing at each other the way they did when we were kids, and they were trying to telepathically communicate with each other. Something was up, but I wasn't sure what. And there was no way I was going to try to figure it out, since my make-a-fool-of-myself jar was full.

"It's nice to meet you, Boone," I said, finally finding my voice and pushing all my emotions to the side. I stood and extended my hand.

Boone glanced up at me before dropping his gaze to my hand and taking it. "You, too."

"I'm Juniper. I guess I'll be training you today."

He nodded and then dropped my hand. "Okay."

I glanced over at Mom and Dad, who were just watching us. I flicked my gaze between them, trying to figure out what their plan was. They looked hopeful as they watched us. It almost felt like they were trying to set us up on a date or something.

But this wasn't the 1800s. My parents knew that would be overstepping and that I would pack my bag so fast if they tried.

So I pushed that worry from my mind and turned my attention back to Boone. I gave him a quick smile as I motioned toward the door. "No time like the present. Let's get working."

I didn't wait for Mom or Dad to respond. I ushered Boone out of Mom's office and showed him where the break room was and where the lockers were for him to put his stuff in. Then I got him a Godwin's vest and led him into the stockroom.

We worked on breaking down the boxes in silence before stacking them into a pile so we could take them out to the recycling bin. By the time the stockroom was cleaned, it was opening time.

Mom came to tell us that she wanted me to check expired products with Boone while she ran the register. I nodded, relieved that she'd given us a task that required very little talking and that allowed us to be a good distance away from each other.

Mindless work was exactly what I needed to get my head right before I went to lunch with Kevin.

Time flew by, and suddenly, my phone was chiming. I climbed down from the ladder I was currently perched on and pulled my phone from my back pocket. My heart picked up speed as I read the text from Kevin.

Kevin: Meet me at Harmony Diner at noon.

I glanced down at my watch. It was 11:45. Harmony Diner was ten minutes walking, which meant I had five minutes to get ready. I glanced in Boone's direction. He was currently heading down his ladder with two cans of black beans in hand. I hurried over to him, and he stopped once his feet were on the ground.

"It's almost time for lunch. I'm going to head to the bathroom to freshen up. I'm meeting someone at the diner. You can order food here or leave as well." I tapped my watch. "Just be back here at one."

He parted his lips to speak, but I didn't have the time. The last thing I wanted to do was get to the diner looking like a mess. I didn't really care what Kevin thought about me. I just didn't want him to use it as evidence that I was a mess without him.

Because I wasn't.

I hurried into the break room and grabbed the bag I'd brought. I shut the bathroom door behind me and stared at my reflection in the mirror. After refreshing my makeup, I took a second to curl the parts of my hair that had gone flat with my cordless curling iron. I glanced down at my watch and cursed. I was going to be late if I didn't leave right now.

I stuffed everything back into the bag and pulled open the bathroom door only to yelp when I saw Mom and Dad standing there. And behind them was Boone, looking very uncomfortable.

I frowned as I looked at him, but he didn't meet my gaze, so I turned to my parents. "What is it?" I asked, trying to ignore the ticking clock in my mind.

Dad looked uneasy, but Mom looked determined, so I knew that I'd already lost. They didn't want me to go to the meeting with Kevin, and I was about to get a fifteen-minute lecture about it.

"Are you heading out?" Mom asked as she raked her gaze over me.

I sighed and pushed my purse strap higher up onto my shoulder. "I'm meeting Kevin in" —I glanced at my watch— "ten minutes."

"Sweetheart, I really don't think you should go. Whatever he has to say can be said over a phone."

"Mom," I said, my tone sharper than I wanted it to be. She needed to realize that I wasn't a teenager anymore. I had a right to go wherever I wanted, with whomever I wanted.

Mom's eyes widened, and I realized that I needed to backpedal. "I know you're worried, but I'll be fine. I promise." I sighed and offered her a soft smile. "It's a public place. Nothing is going to happen to me."

Mom's eyes brimmed with tears, and guilt raged in my stomach. I hated that I worried my mother. I hated that she was reacting this way. I wished that things were easier with Kevin for my parents' sake...but they weren't. I hated that they made me feel like I had to choose.

"Then take Boone with you."

Dad's voice tore through my thoughts. I blinked, turning my attention to Dad. Had I heard him right? "Um, what?"

Dad motioned to Boone, who looked like he wanted to run. "Take Boone with you. If you insist on going despite your mother's wishes, take Boone with you."

Dad kept repeating, *take Boone with you,* like that made it sound less ridiculous. My gaze snapped to Boone.

"Take the guy you just hired? Who I just met? Are you serious?"

Dad faced me, his expression determined. It was in that moment that I realized I'd already lost. I was taking Boone with me whether I wanted to or not.

"Boone doesn't want to come with me," I said, throwing the ball in his court. I waited for him to agree with me as a last-ditch effort to get out of this conversation.

Everyone turned to look at Boone. He glanced between my mom and dad before he shoved his hands into his front pockets and shrugged. "I could eat some food."

I stared at him, willing him to look at me. But he didn't. Instead, he turned his attention to the floor and stood there. Mom glanced back at me with a wide smile.

"There, it's settled. Boone is going with you."

I glanced at my watch and cursed in my mind. I needed to end this conversation and get moving, or I was going to be late. "Fine." I pushed past my parents as I moved out of the break room. "Boone will come with me."

I didn't wait for him to join me as I marched down the hallway and out the back door. I waited to hear it slam shut behind me, but it didn't. Which told me Boone was following me.

I kept my pace as I walked through the back alley of the store and onto Main Street. I didn't stop until I'd pulled open the door to the diner and walked in. A woman was standing at the hostess stand, writing something down on a pad of paper. She looked up as I approached. Her gaze drifted behind me to whom I could only assume was Boone before she smiled at me.

"Table for two?" she asked as she reached down, and two menus suddenly appeared.

"Yes, but not for us two," I said. I pointed behind me. "He's just here to eat by himself."

The hostess studied me and then Boone before she grabbed another menu. "Okay." She turned and motioned for me to follow. "I'll seat you guys over here." She moved past a table full of older Harmony residents.

Some of them I recognized, but I kept my attention forward. I didn't want to get wrapped up in, "I didn't know you were back" conversations.

"Boone Lewis?" One of the men at the table pushed his chair back and stood. "I didn't know you were back, son," he said.

I glanced behind me to see that Boone had stopped to shake the man's hand.

"Are you out of the service now?"

The hostess had stopped at a table a few feet in front of me and was waving her hand toward the table. I wanted to stay and listen to this conversation, but I'd also made it pretty clear to the hostess that Boone and I weren't together. So I forced myself to walk forward, even though my entire being wanted to stay and eavesdrop on the new hire.

"I was honorably discharged," Boone said, his voice quiet.

It felt like the first time I'd heard him speak. I'd pretty much kept to myself while we worked all morning. His voice was smooth, like hot chocolate on a cold Christmas morning. I blinked, feeling strange for having that kind of reaction to a man's voice.

"Is this table okay?" the hostess asked.

I nodded and slipped into the booth. "Thanks."

"Sure. My name is Willow. Let me know if you need anything. Patricia will be your server, and she'll be here shortly."

I took the menu from her. She set the other one in front of me and then moved back to Boone and the older man. After a quick conversation, Boone pulled a chair up to their table and sat down, his focus on the man who had now captivated the attention of everyone around them.

I tried to listen to what they were saying, but I couldn't quite hear. Plus, my nerves were so twisted that I was having a hard time focusing on anything. I swear I could hear the whooshing of blood as my heart pounded.

Where was Kevin? Was he coming, or had he stood me up? Was I an idiot for agreeing to come here?

I felt sick to my stomach, so I sipped the water that Patricia had dropped off before she told me she'd be back when my friend got here. The cool temperature helped take the edge off my anxiety. I set the glass down and looked around. Kevin was nowhere to be found.

I closed my eyes and steadied my breathing. If he didn't come, that was fine. I was going to be fine. I was going to survive. If anything, it would help tonight when I sat at the dinner table with Mom and Dad as they stared at me and then each other as if I couldn't see them. They'd be silently prodding each other to be the first one to ask me a question.

"Hey."

Kevin's deep voice caused me to jump. I yelped, drawing the attention of Boone and the whole table he was sitting with. Boone's gaze was dark as he studied me before he turned to look at Kevin.

Kevin seemed unfazed as he dropped onto the seat across from me. "I'm glad you came," he said. He shifted his weight on the seat and then grinned up at me.

I couldn't untangle the emotions that were rushing through my veins. On the one hand, I was happy to see him. We had a history together. There was something familiar about him that I craved. But the feeling of his hand hitting my face wasn't something I could just forget.

My body stung from the memory of his hands on my body in a way that it hadn't before.

"Juniper, you okay?"

I glanced up to see that he'd dipped down like he was trying to catch my gaze. I swallowed, forcing my emotions to the darkest parts of my mind, and nodded. "Yes, of course," I said, my voice coming out weaker than I wanted it to. I held his gaze and smiled.

He studied me before he nodded and picked up the menu. "Perfect."

Patricia returned to our table and asked Kevin if he wanted something other than water to drink. He asked for a beer, and Patricia nodded before flicking her gaze at me as if to ask if it was okay. I ignored her. Kevin hated it when I asked him not to drink during the day, so I'd learned to stay out of his choices.

Patricia said she'd be back in a few minutes to take our order and left us once more. Kevin turned his attention to me, his smile making me squirm.

"I'm so glad to see you again. I've missed you." He leaned forward to rest his elbows on the table.

I pulled back, pressing my back into the cushions. I didn't like that he was this close or that his sudden movements had me reacting this way. I wanted to tell him to take things slow. That I was going to need time. But the words wouldn't leave my lips.

I couldn't tell him how I felt. I had in the past, but that had always resulted in him hurting me. Or brushing me off like I was some nuisance. I wanted to feel like I could trust him, but...I couldn't.

"Hey, hey," he said as he reached across the table.

I felt his fingers encircle mine before I realized I'd even left my hands on the table. He squeezed my hand before lowering his hand and mine to rest on the tabletop.

"Listen, I know things got heated before. But I was just

upset, that's all." He held my gaze. "You understand why I said what I said."

And did what you did, rushed into my mind, but like always, my tongue felt like cement in my mouth. I couldn't speak, even though I wanted to say so many things.

"That's all over now. Things will be better, I promise." His grip on my hand got tighter and tighter with each word he spoke.

I stared down, trying to process what was happening. My fingers were starting to feel crushed, and my nails were digging into my skin.

"I know you didn't mean to make me upset, which is why I'm willing to forgive you." He smiled again, but it just made bile rise up in my throat. "Just say you won't be like that again, and we can start over new."

I felt frozen in my seat. My mind was screaming at my body to run, but I couldn't move. I couldn't speak. I couldn't react.

"Let her go."

I watched as Kevin glanced to the side. I knew someone was standing there, I'd heard their voice, but I couldn't bring myself to look. It was as if I'd forgotten how to move.

"I said, let her go."

"She's fine." Kevin glanced back at me. "Tell this man you're fine."

I turned to see Boone standing next to the table. His face was like stone as he stared at Kevin, not even bothering to look at me.

"Let her go, and we won't have a problem." Boone took a step closer to Kevin.

I glanced over, warning bells sounding in my mind. But the words to tell Boone what might happen if he provoked Kevin kept slipping away before I could speak them.

Kevin laughed for a few seconds before he grew serious. He dropped my hand and held his up in a mock surrender. "Geez, fine, man. I told you she was okay, but here, I let her go."

Boone glared at him before turning to look at me. "You okay?"

I'd slipped both of my hands into my lap, covering my throbbing one so he couldn't see it. "Yes," I managed to say, hating that I had to lie. But I was afraid of what Boone might do to Kevin, or even worse, what Kevin might do to Boone.

Boone was innocent in all of this. He was forced to come here by my parents. The last thing I needed was for him to end up with a black eye and sue the store.

Boone studied me as if he were willing me to speak. I could feel Kevin's stare; it heated my entire body, so I forced myself to look at Boone.

"I'm fine. We're fine. You can go now." I held his gaze and stilled my facial expression with the hope that he would buy my lie.

"You can go back to your table," Kevin said.

Boone didn't even bother to look over at him. Instead, he studied me before he leaned forward. "I'm just over there."

"Okay." I turned back to Kevin and offered him a smile. "Some people."

Kevin snorted. "Seriously."

Boone paused and glanced down at me before he returned to the table he'd been seated at. I slowly let out the breath that I'd been holding and turned my attention back to Kevin.

I kept the conversation light as Patricia delivered our meal. My stomach was in knots, so I spent most of the time pushing fries around on the plate. I'd ordered a hamburger, but the first bite sank in my stomach like a pile of rocks, so I abandoned it on the edge of my plate.

Kevin didn't seem bothered by our earlier interaction at all. He loved that I kept the conversation focused on him. He sat back, eating and talking like nothing bad had ever happened between us. When Patricia returned to take away the plates, Kevin stood and stretched.

He gave me a kiss on the cheek and told me that he'd call me later before slapping me on the back and walking out of the restaurant. I was left staring at my picked at food and Kevin's empty plate, with a throbbing shoulder and the bill.

Tears stung my eyes as I moved to stand. I grabbed the bill and headed to the hostess stand. Willow wasn't there, so I waited, trying to force myself to get my emotions under control.

"I already paid." Boone's deep voice was close behind me.

I jumped and turned to see him standing there with a

white styrofoam box in his hand. His gaze was dark, and I couldn't quite read it.

"Well, I have to pay," I said as I turned away from him.

Silence.

"Hey, sweetie," an older woman said as she approached the hostess stand. "Your bill's been taken care of. You're free to go."

I blinked a few times as I tried to process her words. Had Kevin paid it without telling me? Had I missed that? I needed to get outside for some fresh air, so I just nodded and turned to hurry from the building.

As soon as I got outside, I walked around the corner and collapsed against the building. The cool of the brick seeped through my clothes, grounding me in the present. I closed my eyes and took long steady breaths through my nose.

"Are you okay?" Boone's voice caused me to open my eyes and glance over my shoulder in his direction.

He was standing about a foot away, just watching me.

"Are you following me now?" I asked, anger spiking. I turned to face him. He didn't know me. He didn't know my situation. He definitely didn't know Kevin. I needed him to stop staring at me like he understood everything. I needed him to...leave.

Boone didn't flinch as I took a step closer to him.

"You're not my big brother. You're not my dad. I don't even know you." Words were tumbling out of my mouth now. "You don't know Kevin. I love him." I was inches away from Boone now, but he didn't pull back. Instead, he just stood there, staring down at me.

"I don't need your help, so go. Now." I pointed my finger toward the road, but Boone didn't flinch. He didn't look. He just stood there, watching me.

Exasperated, I threw my hands up in the air and turned on my heel. "Don't follow me," I called over my shoulder.

But Boone didn't listen. He followed a few feet behind me as I marched back to Godwin's and disappeared inside.

15

CLAIRE

SWEET TEA & SOUTHERN GENTLEMAN

I was an idiot. A big, giant, crazy idiot who let myself get a little too drunk last night, and then...I kissed Jax. I *kissed* Jax.

I asked him to kiss me. I wanted him to kiss me. And I liked it. So much so that I woke up this morning with the memory of his lips on mine forever burned in my mind. I was never going to be the same. That kiss changed me.

Before I came back to Harmony, I could pretend that breaking up with Jax was the right thing to do. I could tell myself that we were better off alone instead of the mess we were together.

But those lies would never overshadow how I felt when he held me last night. Or the way my heart soared when he stared down at me. He made me feel like I was the only woman in the world. That I was his center and he revolved around me.

Until I saw that ring.

That ring hanging from the chain around his neck.

And in that moment, the entire world came crashing down around me. I was just a memory for him, while I was changed forever. He had moved on, and I was never going to be able to. Not since last night. Not since that kiss.

I hated Jax.

"Claire, you haven't said anything."

Brett's voice ripped through my thoughts. I blinked, and the trees outside the large picture window of the apartment I was viewing came back into focus. I turned to see Brett crossing the empty living room to stand next to me. My arms were folded across my chest, and I realized I must have looked upset. I offered him a small smile. "It's nice."

His eyebrows went up. "Really? You like it?"

No. I hated it. I hated everything about this town and the life I was living. I hated that I was never going to be able to go back to just being Claire, the girl who broke up with Jax in high school. I was now something else. I was broken in a way that could never be repaired.

"Yeah, I think it's fine."

Brett's smile made my stomach churn. He looked so happy. He looked like a man in the beginning of a relationship. I knew I should tell him that I was never going to be able to love him. Not while Jax was in the world. But I couldn't bring myself to do that.

I didn't want to be alone. I needed someone in my life who would support me. Heaven knows, Mom would never.

Rose was sick, so I couldn't burden her with my issues. My siblings had their own lives, and I almost never spoke to them. Who could I lean on in this moment?

Brett and I were new. So, while I felt guilty that our relationship was doomed from the beginning, I was okay with sticking around him. After all, we had no labels and no promises that things would progress past what they were currently.

"What does she think?" the leasing agent asked as she stepped up to Brett.

She looked to be our age and was not shy about letting Brett know she was attracted to him. Every question, every comment, was directed at him. I would have been offended if we were really in a relationship, but I wasn't. I was indifferent and distracted.

"I think it's nice," I said, turning to face the two of them. They were standing a few feet off. They both looked up at me.

I glanced around the room. The bare white walls made me sad. "Do you have anything furnished? I don't want to buy all the furniture if I'm only here a little while." I rubbed my upper arm as I swept my gaze around the kitchen and empty dining room, and then back to the leasing agent.

"I'm sorry. All of our furnished apartments are rented out."

"Oh." I sighed as I glanced over at Brett. "I don't know."

He held my gaze before he clapped his hands. "Well,

there's one more place that we can check out that might work."

"I—I just remembered. There's a man moving out next week from a furnished apartment. So, we have one coming available." The leasing agent stumbled over her words.

We both looked over at her, and Brett's smile widened. He glanced at me. "That sounds promising," he said as he crossed the space between us and stopped when he was about a foot in front of me. "That might work."

I sucked in my breath. There was no way that I was going to be able to survive another hour in Jax's house, much less a few days. "Next week?" I asked.

She nodded. "Unless he moves out sooner."

I reached up and rubbed the knot that had formed on the back of my neck ever since Jax knocked on my car window. I slept on it wrong last night, and my whole back felt like it was seizing up. I closed my eyes and let my mind wander. It was either wait until next week or live in an apartment with no furniture.

I could handle being in the same house as Jax. I was a strong, independent woman. I would be fine.

"Okay. Can we go look at it?"

Brett whooped and clapped his hands. He wrapped his arms around me and pulled me to his chest. I stood there, frozen. This was the first time he'd touched me like this, and I wasn't sure what to do about it. It didn't feel right. But then again, I was comparing him to Jax.

Jax was familiar. Jax was a drug that I would never get

enough of. I was certain, with time, Brett would feel the same. I needed to believe that, or I was going to go insane.

It felt strange and robotic, but I wrapped my arms around Brett as he chuckled near my ear. He buried his face in my hair before taking in a deep breath.

"I'm excited for you to live by me. That way, we can get to know each other more." His voice was low and cloaked with meaning.

If I didn't have feelings for Jax, what Brett was doing would have given me butterflies. But with my heart pounding for someone else, his words just annoyed me.

"I'm excited, too," I lied as I patted his back and then moved to step back.

Brett gave me one last squeeze before he released me. Then he turned to the leasing agent and waved toward the door. "Lead the way, m'lady."

We were halfway down the hall when my phone rang. I pulled it from my purse and glanced down. It was Jax.

I stared at his name while my phone vibrated in my hand. My heart was pounding, and my mind was going a million miles a minute. Did I answer? Why was he calling me?

"Who is it? You look like you've seen a ghost." Brett's question pulled me from my trance.

I glanced over at him to see him leaning close to catch a glimpse of my screen. I pressed the side button, and the screen went dark. "It's just Jax."

Brett studied me before he turned and started to walk

down the hallway once again. "You didn't want to take his call?" he asked, tipping his face over his shoulder to catch a glimpse of me.

I shook my head. "I'm sure it's nothing." I gave him a quick smile and quickened my step to catch up with him.

We walked in silence for a few seconds before I felt Brett's gaze on me. I could see his quizzical stare from the corner of my eye. I glanced over at him before drawing my eyebrows together. "What?"

"Is there, like, something going on between the two of you?"

My blood ran cold, but thankfully, my brain didn't miss a beat. "Jax and me?"

He nodded. "Like, I know you said it was in the past. But..." He raised his eyebrows.

I knew what he was asking and what he wanted me to say. But I didn't know how to voice the words. So I asked him something instead. "Why would you wear a necklace with a woman's ring on it?"

He frowned. "I don't."

I waved away his answer. "I don't mean *you*, you. Why would a man wear the ring of a woman around his neck?"

"Are we talking about Jax?" He must have seen my exaggerated expression because he nodded. "Um, okay. Probably because I didn't want to forget her." Then he shook his head. "More like he can't forget her."

My stomach dropped to my feet. I'd known the reason, I just needed to hear it from someone else. I needed to hear a man confirm to me what I'd thought all along. Jax hadn't gotten over whoever wore that ring in his past.

I was the only idiot who continued to hang on.

"Jax and I are over. There's nothing between us."

Just as the last word left my lips, my phone rang once again. We both glanced down as Jax's name flashed on the screen. I glanced up to Brett, who met my gaze. There was a daring look in his eyes. One that said, *prove it*.

I steeled my nerves and pressed the talk button. I pressed the phone to my ear and turned away from Brett, who moved to talk to the leasing agent a few feet off.

"Hello?" I asked, hating that my heart was pounding. Could Brett hear it? Could Jax?

"Why didn't you answer?" he asked.

I pinched the bridge of my nose and closed my eyes. "Sorry, it stopped ringing by the time I got to it," I lied. "What did you need?"

"Carmel's in labor. She's birthed two puppies, but now nothing is happening. I'm trying to help, but I don't know what I'm doing."

All the clouds that had formed in my mind since last night lifted, and my body sprang into action. I told Jax that I was leaving right now. I hung up on him before he could say anything. I slipped my phone into my purse as I hurried over to Brett.

"We have to go. Now," I said as I barreled past him and down the hallway to the stairs.

Brett was sputtering behind me. I knew he was

confused, but I didn't stop to answer questions. I pressed the door release, and the bright afternoon sun assaulted my eyes. I lifted my hand to lessen the sting just as Brett caught up with me.

"What's wrong?" he asked as he pulled his car keys from his pocket.

I waved toward his car. "My dog is in labor. We have to get back to Jax's house." I half walked, half sprinted to the passenger door and pulled it open as soon as I heard the locks release.

I slipped onto the seat and buckled myself in while Brett did the same. He started the engine and peeled out of the parking lot. We drove in silence, the seconds ticking by like molasses. By the time he pulled into Jax's driveway, I was so wound up that I wanted to spring out of the car.

My hand was on the door handle, but the lack of movement on Brett's part had me stop. I glanced over, expecting to see him turn off his car and come in, but he didn't move.

He met my gaze. "Listen, I don't really do dogs." He paused. "Or birth." He gave me an apologetic smile. "So, call me when you get done?"

I didn't have time to digest his words or to beg him to come with. I didn't want to be alone with Jax, but I also didn't want to force him to be with me. I just nodded and pulled on the handle. "Okay."

I stepped out onto the driveway when I heard Brett call, "Wait."

I glanced down to see him leaning forward with an

earnest look in his eye. "Let me know if there's anything you need me to bring you. I'm happy to be the courier."

"I will," I said as I stepped back and slammed the door.

I sprinted across the driveway and up the front steps, where I pulled open the door. Once inside, I frantically searched the house for Jax. I found him on the kitchen floor with Carmel lying prone on the ground. I could hear the soft whimpers of puppies, but Jax's shoulders were tense.

"I'm here," I breathed out as I dropped down next to Jax. He had her tail pulled up and was feeling around the birth canal.

The look in his eyes told me something was wrong. Really wrong.

"I think a puppy is stuck. And no matter how much I try to help, nothing is happening." He squinted like he was trying to feel for something. "Poor girl is exhausted," he said as he reached forward with his free hand and rubbed Carmel's belly.

That act alone would have elicited an excited tail wag from Carmel in the past, but she didn't move her head or her body to acknowledge his touch.

"We need to get her to the vet," I whispered, fear and emotions clinging to every surface of my body.

Jax nodded.

We worked in silence. We wasted no time gathering everything up. I was in charge of the puppies while Jax wrapped Carmel in a blanket and scooped her up. I led the way, holding the front door open so he could come through.

I then quickly let it shut behind me as I hurried to open the truck door.

I sat in back with Carmel lying next to me. The two puppies were squeaking and searching for their momma while they rested on my lap. I kept my hand on Carmel's head, scratching her just below the ears—her favorite.

Jax pulled into the parking lot at the vet's and turned the engine off. He got out and pulled open the back door to hoist Carmel out. I followed behind him as we hurried into the vet's office.

"We need help," he called as soon as he was through the doors. "My dog, she's in labor, but I think a puppy is stuck."

The receptionist leapt into action. She waved for Jax to follow her through the exam room and into the back surgery room. She had him lay Carmel down on a steel table just as the vet and a tech came into the room.

The tech took the puppies from my hands while the vet started his assessment. The receptionist moved to face us and told us that it was best to let them work before she ushered us out of the room.

It wasn't until I was sitting on a chair in the waiting room that the adrenaline in my body started to dissipate. It was quiet, the only sound was some soft music coming from the receptionist's desk. Jax had left to go wash his hands in the bathroom, and I was alone.

My body started to shake as I realized that I could lose my dog. Besides Rose, she was the only person in town who was happy to see me. I'd promised to care for her and protect her, but I'd failed.

Tears started to flow, so I leaned forward, resting my elbows on my knees so I could bury my face in my hands. If Carmel died, I wasn't sure what I was going to do. I needed her to live.

"Hey, hey," Jax's soft voice broke through my sobs.

His hands surrounded mine, and he gently pulled them back. He knelt down in front of me, so his gaze could meet mine. All I saw in his eyes was compassion and care. He was just as worried about Carmel as I was.

He held my gaze for a moment before he stood and then pulled me up as well. I didn't stop him as he wrapped his arms around me and drew me to his chest. He smelled familiar. He felt familiar. The way he rested his chin on the top of my head was familiar.

He felt like home when I was so desperate for a place to land. I hated that he was my lighthouse in the dark, but I couldn't deny it anymore. He was the person I was made to love, even if he loved someone else.

He was what I needed to breathe. What I needed to survive.

I wasn't sure how long we stood there, embracing. But Jax didn't seem to want to stop, and I wasn't ready to let go. Eventually, another patient came in, and we pulled apart at the sound of the bells on the front door jingling. Jax kept his gaze ahead as he stepped back. I wasn't sure where to look or what to say, so I just sat back down on the chair.

After a few seconds, Jax sat down next to me.

Silence filled the space between us. I so badly wanted to reach over and entwine my fingers with his. But I didn't. We weren't a couple.

Finally, I breathed a sigh of relief when the vet came out. He was smiling, which I took as a good sign.

"Carmel will be fine," he said as he approached us. "She's sedated now, but she will be okay."

I let out my breath and stood, tears of joy filling my eyes.

"However, we lost the three babies that had yet to be born."

My heart ached for the ones we lost and for Carmel. "The other two?"

"Loud and hungry."

I smiled. It wasn't the best scenario, but I would take it.

"Can I see her?" I asked stepping toward the door that the vet had just come through.

"Sure," he said, turning toward the receptionist. "Robin, can you take Ms. Hodges back to see Carmel?"

She nodded and stood up from her chair. When she rounded the desk, she motioned toward the door. "You can follow me here."

Jax said that he would wait for me, and the vet moved to greet the tiny woman and large rottweiler that had just come in. I followed close behind Robin as she led me to the back cages where Carmel was sleeping. She was curled up on some blankets, heavily sedated.

I took my time burying my face into the fur on her head

while scratching her ears and whispering that I was sorry. I closed my eyes and breathed in deep, smiling at the sound of her puppies rooting around her mid-section.

"She should be able to go home tomorrow," the vet tech said as she stepped closer to join me.

I glanced over to see her soft smile that caused crinkles to form around her eyes. "Really?"

She nodded. "We want her to stay the night for observation, but you can come get her tomorrow."

"Okay," I whispered as I turned my attention back to Carmel. Her eyes were closed, and she looked peaceful, so I took a step back, letting the vet tech close the door to the kennel.

Then she turned to face me and smiled once more.

"I should probably go," I said, my voice cloaked in exhaustion.

"You can call anytime if you get worried."

I nodded. "I will probably do that later, so expect it."

The vet tech laughed. "You wouldn't be the first one."

She directed me on how to get back to the front desk. When I got out there, Robin was sitting at her desk again. The realization that I was going to have a big, fat bill rammed me like a freight train.

I made my way up to Robin's desk and rested my arm on the ledge in front of her. I didn't know how to ask if there was a payment plan without sounding like a loser, so I just stood there, staring at her.

"Everything okay?" she asked as she looked up from her computer.

I sucked in my breath. It was now or never. "Do you have a payment plan option by chance?"

Robin studied me before turning to her computer. "Carmel's bill has actually been paid."

I frowned. "It has?"

She nodded before she looked over at Jax. "In full, just a few minutes ago."

I didn't want to look or acknowledge, but I had a sinking feeling as to who the generous donor was.

"Did you pay?" I asked, as I tipped my face toward Jax without meeting his gaze.

"Me?" He pointed at his chest. "No."

I was confused. I furrowed my brow as I glanced back at Robin, who had been watching Jax.

She snapped her gaze to me and nodded. "It's true. It wasn't him." She leaned forward and studied her computer monitor. "It was a Brett Morris who called in and paid the bill."

"Brett?" His name left my lips, but my brain hadn't caught up. "Brett paid?" I stared at the ledge in front of me. "Huh."

"Do you know him?" Robin asked.

I nodded.

"Is this a surprise?"

"Total."

Brett had paid for Carmel's surgery? I did not expect

that. Maybe I had been wrong about him. Maybe I needed to give him a second look. If Jax had moved on with necklace girl, maybe I could move on with Brett. It was a possibility, and right now, I had no other options.

He could make me happy. Even if I wasn't even sure how to be that anymore.

16
JAX

SWEET TEA &
SOUTHERN GENTLEMAN

M y truck was silent as I drove Claire back to my
house. I hated that her eyes lit up when Robin told
her that Brett had paid for the vet bill. It didn't have
anything to do with the fact that I had actually been the one
to take care of it—I just hated that she *wanted* him to be the
one who took care of her.

She was going to ride into the sunset with that fool, and
I was yet again going to be the one left behind, unable to
move on and clinging to memories we shared. This was my
fate. It was cruel and torturous, but I didn't know how to let
her go.

And I didn't think that I was ever going to be able to.

I wanted to ask her how her apartment search went. I
wanted to ask when she was moving out, so I could finally be
alone to lick my wounds, but the words just wouldn't form
on my tongue.

So I gripped the steering wheel like it owed me money. I kept my gaze focused on the road in front of me as my body took over and I went into autopilot.

From the corner of my eye, I could see Claire peeking over at me every so often. She would study me for a moment before she dropped her gaze to her hands. Then, a few seconds later, she would look over at me once more.

My jaw muscles flinched every time she looked at me. I could tell that she wanted to say something to me, but I wasn't ready to hear it.

I wasn't certain that I could hear it.

We had a few hours before we needed to be at the pub to open it. All I wanted to do right now was go home, work with my hands, and then shower. Fishing had been relaxing for the small amount of time that I'd done it. But then Gramps called and told me that something was wrong with Carmel, so I rushed home.

I didn't have the time I needed to clear my head, like I so desperately needed to. If I didn't take the time, I was certain that I was going to explode and do something stupid. Like pull Claire into my arms and not let her go until I showed her exactly how I felt about her. I was moments away from breaking down all of my walls just for a chance to let her in.

Even if she burned my heart to the ground, it would be worth it to feel her once more. To remind myself of what it was like to be the only one who could love her. Who could touch her.

That desire was growing stronger by the second, and my resolve to keep it at bay was waning.

I was born to love Claire. No matter how many times she pushed me away. Or how many times she told me we could never be anything more. I didn't care. I wanted her to be mine.

Forever.

I cursed in my mind, pushing my ridiculous thoughts from my head and took the left into my driveway. I pulled in and saw Claire's busted-down car a few feet off. I knew what I was going to do to keep my mind off this frustrating woman.

I was going to fix her car even though she didn't want me to touch it. I didn't care. I needed this for myself.

I put my truck in park and pulled the keys out as I opened the driver's door and got out. The sound of the passenger door opening and gravel crunching under her feet told me she was out, but I forced myself to keep my gaze focused on my closed garage door. I was going to get my tools and get lost in a world that made sense. A car engine.

"I, um..."

Claire's voice caused me to stop in my tracks. I wanted to turn around to look at her, but I couldn't bring myself to. If I did, then I wouldn't be able to stop. I would break, and I wasn't ready for that.

"Thanks."

I cleared my throat and nodded. "I did it for Carmel."

"I know," she said quickly.

I winced, hating how convincing her tone sounded. Could she not tell that I was lying? I did that—I did everything—for her. I'd spent so many years waiting for her to come home to me. To realize that whatever family feud she thought our families were in, I didn't care.

I picked her. I would *always* pick her. Everything else could burn to the ground.

"I think I'll take a shower. Just let me know when you want to leave for the pub."

I closed my eyes as my mind went to the seventh level of hell. Why did she tell me that she was going to take a shower? Now, I was going to be stuck with images of her standing under the water with soap slipping down her soft, creamy skin.

I growled as I made my way to the side door to the garage and pulled it open. I needed to do something with my hands before my desire for her took over and I threw caution to the wind. I slammed my fist against the garage door opener, and thankfully, by the time the door retracted, she was gone.

My entire body felt hot, so I pulled my t-shirt off and threw it onto my worktable. I lost myself in popping the hood of her car and assessing the situation. I was under her car, sweat dripping off my skin, when I heard the soft sound of her clearing her throat.

I closed my eyes, thankful that the work had distracted me long enough to regain a semblance of sanity, but now, it was all for naught. I could see her legs as she stood next to the car. She must have finished her shower and come out here to give me a tongue-lashing for going against her wishes.

Because she didn't *trust* me. Even though she trusted me enough to live in my house, leave her dog with me, and sleep in the room next to mine.

Realizing that I was stalling, I took in a deep breath and pushed out from under her car. The sun was behind her, so I had to squint to make her out. Her hair was down and curled, framing her face. She was wearing a floral dress that hit just above her knee, and the neckline scooped down so low that it had my mouth turning dry.

"What are you doing?" she asked as she shifted so I could see her better.

I hated that I couldn't think when she was around me. I hated that she seemed relaxed while I felt as if my entire body was on a spring about to pop off at any moment. And I hated that she didn't seem bothered by our kiss last night. I doubted she even remembered it.

I tossed the towel that I'd been wiping my hands off with to the side and stood. I didn't realize how close Claire had been standing to me until I was on my feet. Her eyes widened as I stared down at her. I knew I should pull back. Being this close to her could have dire consequences if the dam that kept my feelings at bay broke. But I didn't move. I enjoyed seeing her squirm. I enjoyed seeing her gaze dip to my chest for a moment before it came back up to meet mine.

"I'm fixing your car," I said, my voice deep and daring. I

wanted her to pick this fight. I was tired of playing her games. She was going to know how I felt about her even if I couldn't say the words.

"But..."

I turned away from her and headed into the garage. If she didn't want me doing this, she was going to have to stop me. I grabbed a wrench and headed back out to her car. She was still standing where I'd left her. She had one arm wrapped around her stomach and rested the other elbow on her forearm so she could chew on her thumbnail.

"Let it go, Claire," I said as I walked past her.

She startled and looked over at me. I met her gaze for a moment before I dropped down to the ground to scoot back under her car.

"Letting me fix your car isn't going to kill you." I shifted my weight back and forth until I was back to the spot I'd been before.

Now that she could no longer see me, I dropped my head and closed my eyes. I waited for her to leave, and it felt like an eternity before she turned and disappeared.

I spent the next hour fixing her car. Once I was certain that I'd found the issue and resolved it, I gathered my tools and brought them back into the garage. I put them away, closed the garage door, and headed to her car to close the hood. I was sweaty and covered in grease—I needed a shower.

Claire must have been in the spare room. When I got inside, she was nowhere to be seen. I headed into my bathroom with a towel and spent a good fifteen minutes under the hot water, cursing myself for falling, once more, for the woman from my past.

Once I was cleaned and dressed, I grabbed my keys and wallet and opened my bedroom door. I headed down the hallway, but when I got to Claire's door, I paused. I turned to face it, raising my hand to knock, but feeling frozen.

Before I could move, her door opened, and she appeared in front of me. Her gaze caught mine, and her eyes widened as she stared at me. She stood there, not moving.

"Jax," she whispered as her gaze drifted to my raised hand before coming back to study me. "Have you been standing here long?"

I cleared my throat and forced my mind to focus. "Time to go," I said before I turned and headed down the hallway.

I could hear her footsteps behind me. I could feel her presence even though she wasn't touching me. She was going to haunt me the rest of my life no matter what I did. I couldn't run away from her.

And I didn't want to.

I didn't have to ask if she was going to ride with me; she just made her way to the passenger door and climbed into my truck. She knew that her car was fixed, but she still wanted to ride with me. I hated and loved that at the same time.

I kept my distance once we got to the pub. We had an hour before it opened. Remus and Henry were already there, getting things ready. I had Claire wipe down the tables while I readied the bar for tonight. Remus could tell that I was in a mood. He kept glancing over at me, but all I had to do was tell him to drop it once, and he didn't ask me any of the questions I could see he was desperate to ask.

Fifteen minutes to open, I turned on the music and dimmed the lights. Claire was sitting at a booth, swiping on her phone. I wanted to ask if she was talking to Brett, but I didn't want the answer I was sure would come. So I just stood behind the bar, glaring at everything in front of me.

Thankfully, the pub filled quickly, and I was so busy that I didn't have time to think about Claire. I'd gathered enough strength to only look at her every few minutes. It wasn't perfect, but I was getting stronger.

A few hours after open, Abigail, Shelby, Sabrina, and a woman I didn't recognize walked into the pub. I heard Claire squeal as she hurried to put down the black tray she'd just used to deliver food to a table of construction workers, before she rushed over to them. They all hugged, and Claire ushered them to an empty table in the back.

I pulled my attention from them to find Remus watching me. I glared at him, and he just raised his eyebrows. "You're going to set something on fire with a look like that," he said as he filled a Coke and gave it to Mrs. Sanderson. She thanked him and threw a few dollars into the tip jar.

"Drop it," I growled as I took a twenty from a man I didn't recognize and opened the cash drawer. I handed the man his change and gave him a quick smile before turning back to Remus.

"Geez, man. The faster Claire leaves, the better," he said as he met my gaze head-on. "She should have never come back."

"Stop," I spat. I loved my best friend, but sometimes he stepped over the line. He was dangerously close to saying something that I wasn't going to tolerate.

"Come on, man. She walks all over you. Look at her. She's not even working. If she was actually on the payroll, you would have fired her."

My gaze snapped to Claire, who was now sitting at the table with her friends talking. Anger and pain rose in my stomach. Was Remus right? Did Claire just take advantage of me? She didn't care about my feelings. And she didn't see me as a boss. I was always there, ready and waiting to take care of her.

I didn't respond to Remus. Instead, I turned and walked out from behind the bar. I didn't stop—I didn't think—as I made my way to the table and stood next to Claire. She glanced up at me, her smile fading as she studied my face.

"Can I talk to you?" I asked, nodding my head toward the door that led to the kitchen.

She glanced around at the other women at the table and then back to me. "Um, sure."

I turned and headed toward the doors, not waiting to see if she was going to follow me. I pushed through the swinging doors and stood next to the wall. My nerves were shot, and I was ready for her to move on, so I could heal. Or at least pretend that she had never come, and I wasn't heartbroken.

"What do you need?" she asked as she pushed through the doors and her gaze found mine.

"Do I need to remind you that you work for me?"

Her eyebrows went up. "What?"

I waved my hand around the kitchen. "You are here to work, not to socialize."

Her cheeks flushed, and she crossed her arms. "I know that. It's just that Abigail got engaged, so she was telling me the story."

I shook my head. "I don't care. You're here to wait tables, not chat with your friends. I know you're leaving, but you're still in my house, taking up my space and eating my food. The least you can do is fulfill your end of the bargain." I walked around her and headed to the swinging doors. "I fulfilled mine."

I didn't wait for her answer as I pushed back out into the pub. The doors swung shut behind me. I headed to the bar once more, where I started to fill orders. A few minutes later, I saw the swinging doors open and Claire emerge. Her lips were drawn taut, and her eyes looked dark as she surveyed the room. After taking a new table's order, she headed over to the table with her friends. She took their order and promptly left.

When she got to the bar, she handed me their drink requests. "I'll be paying for them," she said, not meeting my gaze. She was gone before I could respond, so I filled their orders and left them on a black tray on the bar.

We worked like this the rest of the night. Speaking but not really talking to each other. Her friends lingered for about an hour before they left, making a point to tell her goodbye. Half an hour before close, Remus clapped me on the shoulder and wished me good luck.

Thankfully, there were no lingering drunks when closing time came, so I was able to lock the door right at two. Claire was doing some dishes in the back, so I turned on my music and got lost in washing the glass tumblers and wine glasses at the bar.

Eventually, Claire came into the pub with a broom in hand. She started sweeping against the far wall and slowly made her way toward the bar. Her hips were swaying to the music, and I couldn't help but stare at the way her body moved. When she tipped her head back, exposing her neck and the creamy skin over her clavicle, I flipped the music off.

This was torture, and it was killing me.

Claire glanced over at me and frowned. I ignored her as I continued to wash the glasses and stack them on a towel I'd laid out on the bar.

"Did I do something wrong?" she asked.

I glanced up to see that she was standing next to the bar now. She'd abandoned the broom and had her hands firmly planted on her hips. I studied her for a moment before I shrugged. "I was just done listening to the music, that's all."

I could tell she didn't believe me, and she wasn't going to let that be my excuse.

"You've been short and rude to me all night. I didn't mean to break your rules when the girls came in. Abigail just got engaged. I was happy for her." She glowered at me. "You know, happy? It seems to be a feeling you are incapable of."

Heat pricked my collar as I stared at her. Happy? How was I supposed to feel happy with her constantly leaving? I was the one who stayed. I was the one who was constant.

When I didn't answer her right away, she blew out her breath and looked around. "So, you're mad that I'm at your house? Or is it because I'm eating your food?" She turned on her heel and marched through the swinging doors.

My gaze followed her, wondering what she was doing, but a few seconds later, she returned with her wallet in her hand. "Or did you think I won't pay for the drinks?" She pulled out a few twenties and threw them down on the table.

I shook my head and pushed the money back to her. "It was on the house. I'm happy for Abigail."

Claire stared at me before dropping her gaze to the money. Then she picked it up and pushed it toward me once more. "Take the money, Jax. Take it. I don't want this to come back and bite me in the butt when you're unhappy and want yet another reason to hate me."

I studied her before my gaze dropped to the money in her outstretched hand. I was drying a tumbler, so my hands were too preoccupied to take anything from her.

She mumbled under her breath as she made a fist, crumpling the bills. She turned toward the swinging doors and marched through them. I smirked, enjoying the fact I'd won this battle, even though I was losing the war.

I'd just set down a dry tumbler when Claire returned. I turned to gloat only to see her holding a small piece of paper that looked like a receipt. She was staring at it, her lips parted, like she wasn't sure what she was looking at.

I realized what had just happened. She must have gone to my office to put the money in my wallet and found the receipt.

The receipt for the vet.

"Claire—"

"Jax, what is this?"

17

CLAIRE

SWEET TEA & SOUTHERN GENTLEMAN

My body felt numb. My hand was shaking, and my heart was pounding so loud that I could hear the whooshing sound of blood as it pumped through my ears. I was angry and confused at the same time, yet all I could do was stand in front of Jax with my hand outstretched, staring at him. Waiting for him to explain himself.

"What is this?" I repeated as I inwardly willed his gaze to meet mine.

Jax didn't look up. Instead, he kept his gaze focused on the tumbler that he'd just set down.

I smoothed out the receipt and set it down next to the tumbler. He had to acknowledge it now. I watched as his gaze flicked to the white paper, and in one quick motion, he grabbed it, crumpled it in his hand, and tossed it into the garbage behind the bar.

It took a moment for my mind to catch up with what

just happened. Anger pricked at my neck as I stared at him. He didn't just do that...did he?

Instead of looking up and acknowledging me, he grabbed the dish towel and turned to face the sink. He turned the water on and began to rinse another tumbler.

"So, you're just not going to talk to me?" I asked as I walked around the bar and approached him. "Did you ask the vet to lie about who paid for Carmel's bill?"

I was a foot away from Jax now. I watched as his entire body stiffened as if he'd suddenly realized that I was standing so close to him.

He had nowhere to go. He had to acknowledge me and my questions. Why wouldn't he just tell me the truth?

"Why would you have them lie?"

I watched as Jax tipped his head ever so slightly in my direction before he flung the dish towel onto his shoulder and sidestepped me. He grabbed a grey tub that was sitting on the bar and went to gather the dishes that were scattered around the room.

I was spitting mad. Not only was he ignoring me, but now he was literally running away from me. I wasn't going to let him get away from this conversation. He was going to answer me if it was the last thing he did.

"I just don't understand you. You tell me that I'm nothing but a burden to you. That I take up your space. That I eat your food. You act like a jerk to me when I'm around my friends, but then you do something like this. Why would you let me believe that Brett was the one who paid for Carmel?" My mind was reeling and going a mile a minute. My mouth didn't seem to have a problem keeping up with my thoughts.

"Unless..." Realization dawned on me. "You realized that if I didn't have the money to pay for Carmel, I would stay in Harmony longer, and I would have to keep working for you. Paying for Carmel is just your way of getting rid of me faster."

My heart plummeted to the floor as the words left my lips. I was the only one who had felt something that night. I was the only one who still cared. Jax was just doing these things to make it easier for me to go.

Jax had stopped moving. He was staring straight ahead, his entire body frozen. I'd hit the nail on the head. His body language proved it.

I was the idiot who wanted to be with him. He was the idiot who wanted me to leave.

Tears pricked my eyes as my heart once again was being pulled from my chest and pulverized in the blender that Jax used to make drinks. I was the only one who had held on to what we had before, like it was special.

I was the idiot who had hoped for something more.

"What's the point?" Jax's voice was hushed, and for a moment, I wondered if I'd imagined him speaking.

"What?" I asked, leaning in.

"I said, what's the point?" His voice had dropped an octave.

I frowned as his words rolled around in my head. "What's the point of what?"

He glanced over his shoulder, and his gaze met mine. His eyes were a dark, stormy blue as he stared at me. "What's the point of trying? You and me?" He turned toward me now and flicked his finger from his chest to me. "Fate has decided, and we lost."

His words stung. He'd taken my open and bleeding heart and doused it with rubbing alcohol, like that was what I needed to heal. I didn't need him to tell me that trying to be something with him was pointless. I needed him to tell me that he'd moved on. That he didn't love me. Not that he couldn't fathom the work it would take to make us happen.

He held my gaze before dropping it and studying the floor. "It's better for us to move on. There's no point in trying to make something work between us. Our ship has sailed, and we should accept that." He shoved his hands into his front pockets and shrugged. "You're better off with someone like Brett. And I..."

I hated him in this moment. I hated that he wasn't fighting for us. That he'd just given up and resigned himself to a future without me. Suspicion that he was saying this to let me down easy grew in my mind. He wanted to be free to love the woman whose ring he had hanging from his neck. He just couldn't say the words.

He was a coward.

"And you with the girl whose ring you can't seem to get

rid of?" I spat out with more malice in my voice than I'd intended.

Jax's eyes widened as if I'd just slapped him.

"What?" he asked.

"You're ridiculous, you know that? Always lying. Always twisting the truth in your favor. I should have never trusted you. I should have never fallen in love with you. I was the fool. You turned out to be exactly who my mom said you were." Tears were flowing down my cheeks now, and I hated that there was nothing I could do to stop them.

The truth was, I still loved Jax. I loved him more than anything. But he was never going to love me. He had secrets, and he was never going to show me his real self.

I turned and hurried across the bar to the swinging door. I needed to get out of here. The walls were closing in on me, and I couldn't breathe. I couldn't think. I needed to find a cool, dark place where I could hide out until my anger for Jax replaced my broken heart and I could think again.

"Claire!" A warm hand grabbed my elbow, halting my retreat.

I didn't turn around even though my whole body responded to the feeling of his skin against mine. Electricity raced up my arm and exploded throughout my whole chest. Was I always going to feel this way about him? Was I ever going to be able to move on?

Was I doomed to love a man who would never love me back?

What did I do in my previous lives to deserve this kind of heartbreak?

I closed my eyes and stilled my body. I took in a deep breath before I whispered, "What do you want from me, Jax?"

He released my arm, but I could still feel his presence. I was always going to be able to feel him as he stood next to me. My body couldn't seem to forget what it felt like to be touched by him. To be held by him...to be kissed by him.

"Do you..." His voice was quiet and unsure. Like he wasn't quite ready to ask me the question that lingered in his mind. "Do you remember the kiss?" He paused. "I thought you were too drunk to remember."

I closed my eyes and shook my head. "What does it matter? We can never seem to be honest with each other." A black cloud settled in my heart as I resigned myself to what Jax had said earlier. What was the point? Fate hated the two of us being together. Why were we fighting to fit together something that could never fit?

"What does that mean?" Jax's words were so sharp that I turned to look at him. His eyebrows were drawn together as if he were trying to understand what I'd just said.

I sighed as I wiped the lingering tears from my cheeks. He had to know what I was talking about. Our family. His mom. My dad. *My* mom. So many hurt feelings. So many lies. We were fools to think that we could sustain a relationship through it all.

"Why can't we be honest with each other?" He dipped

down in an attempt to catch my gaze. It worked. He locked eyes with me, and I felt helpless to pull away. "Are you not honest with me?"

I shook my head. I'd always been honest with him...until Mom told me that he would do anything to hurt our family. Then I pulled away. But I never lied.

I just didn't know how to ask him how he could have lied to me. I didn't want him to say that everything I held dear, the relationship I imagined we had, wasn't real.

I didn't want to hear that.

I couldn't stand there with him staring at me and my heart pounding like it wanted to sprint free from my chest. I needed to get out of here.

I turned and headed toward the swinging doors once more. Once again, his hand found my elbow, but this time, he didn't just turn me around. He pulled me over to the wall next to the door. He caged me in with his hands on either side of my head.

His body leaned in but didn't touch mine. He was making it impossible for me to run away again.

"Tell me what you're thinking, Claire." His voice had dropped to a desperate whisper. His gaze never left my face. I was staring at his chest as he took deep breaths, expanding and contracting. "You owe me the truth. After you left me hanging that night, I deserve to hear why you threw me away like a piece of garbage."

Tears pricked my eyes once more. I didn't want to say the words because I didn't want to hear the truth. That he'd never loved me. That our relationship had been a lie. That it had been some sick way to hurt my family. I wasn't going to be able to survive a blow like that.

But when I finally met his gaze, the dam inside of me broke. I needed closure on this part of my life, and if speaking the words out loud was the way to get the peace my soul needed, then I was going to say everything.

The words began to tumble from my lips. I told him everything. I told him what my mom said. I told him about my dad. I told him that I believed he'd only pretended to love me.

I thought he would pull back. I thought a smile would creep across his lips in acknowledgement of his master plan. At least, that was what the villain always did in the movies. To hear their plan spoken out loud by the person they harmed the most always seemed to give them a sense of satisfaction.

But Jax didn't look happy. His lips were turned down into a frown, and the look in his eyes was one of confusion as I stood there, yelling at him. I was so worked up that my entire body was shaking. When the last few words left my lips, I collapsed against the wall, grateful that Jax had pulled me to it.

I covered my face with my hands and cried. I was emotionally spent. I'd spent so long holding my frustrations in, that I didn't know who I was without them. But they were spoken into the ether and there was no way to get them back.

I was alone.

Jax sighed. "I don't know what you are talking about. I didn't know about my mom and your dad. I don't know about some game your mom thinks we're playing. I loved you, Claire. I was ready to do whatever it took to be with you."

His words filled my head, but I kept my face covered, unable to look at him. I wanted to believe what he was saying, but I wasn't sure who I could trust anymore.

"The feud between our families is ridiculous. Your mom thinks we're plotting and planning to take her down, but the truth is, we have our own family problems to sort through. We don't care what the Hodgeses are doing."

I peeked at him through my fingers. He'd pushed off the wall and was pulling out the necklace with the offending ring hanging from it. He unclasped the chain and slid the ring onto his palm. He stuffed the empty chain into his pocket and returned to resting one hand next to my head while the other one held the ring up for me to inspect.

"You were right about one thing." His voice sent shivers down my back.

I pulled my hands away from my face and wiped my tears with my fingertips. I was too tired to cry anymore, and I was ready to hear about this girl he couldn't seem to move on from.

"I can't get rid of this ring. Because I can't move on from the girl that this ring belonged to."

This was good. Even though my heart was breaking, I needed this for closure.

"She's beautiful. Her dark hair. Her soulful eyes. Her love for animals. The way she makes me laugh. The way she makes me want to be a better man." His gaze slowly lifted from the ring to my lips.

"Her kisses make me weak. Her body awakens mine. She's the missing puzzle piece in my life. I don't know how to breathe without her. When she's away, I'm not whole, I'm not the man I'm supposed to be." His gaze slowly lifted to meet mine.

"Then why aren't you with her?" I choked out. This was a special kind of torture.

"I want to be with her." He held my gaze. "But she doesn't seem to want me."

I frowned. Who wouldn't want Jax?

He sighed. "You're a smart girl, Claire. But right now, you're being incredibly dense." I parted my lips, but he just shook his head. "This was the ring I was going to give you the night you stood me up." He wiggled the ring under my nose. "This is yours, goddammit."

My gaze snapped from the ring to his gaze. His eyebrows were knit together like saying those words exposed a wound he'd spent years trying to cover.

"Mine?" I whispered. "Why?"

He pressed in, his chest mere inches from mine. "Because I love you. I've never stopped loving you." He dropped the ring into his palm before fisting it so he could use the pad of his forefinger to lift my chin.

I watched as his gaze dropped to my lips before slowly lifting to hold my gaze once more.

"I was made to love you, Claire Hodges. I can't love anyone else." He sighed. "I've tried to move on, but I can't seem to make anything stick. So I waited. I waited for you to come back. I waited for you to finally love me."

The rush of joy I felt every time he said the word *love* had my entire body thrumming with pleasure. He loved me, and I...loved him.

My hands found his waist, and his muscles twitched. His eyes widened as he glanced down to watch my hands move from his abs up to his chest before they settled on his shoulders. I stepped closer to him, bringing our bodies within centimeters of each other.

His gaze didn't soften. The worry lines between his brows deepened. I lifted a hand and ran the tips of my fingers over them.

"Do you love me, Claire?" He whispered as his hands found my waist and he drew me into him. The heat of his palms seeped through my clothes and emanated throughout my body.

My gaze dropped to his as my hand moved to cup his cheek. I rose up onto my tiptoes and brushed my lips across his. His grip tightened on my waist, and his eyes closed.

"I love you," I whispered.

He pulled me the rest of the way, crashing our bodies together. He captured my lips with his. My hand went to the nape of his neck as I threaded my fingers through his hair.

He dropped down so he could wrap his arms around my waist and pull me off my feet. I wrapped my legs around his waist as he pressed me against the wall, freeing one hand to use as support.

I parted my lips and let him in. His tongue danced around mine as we deepened the kiss. My fingers moved from his neck to his chest, down till I found the bottom of his shirt and began to play with the hem.

He growled as he moved his hands to support my rear and carried me through the swinging doors and down the hall. He didn't stop until we were in his office. He used a free hand to swipe the items on his desk to the floor before he sat me down. With his hands now free, he pulled back, so he could cup my face.

I whimpered, missing the feeling of his lips on mine. But the intensity of his gaze caused my whole body to still.

"I love you," he whispered.

"I love you, too."

His hand slid from my cheek, down my left arm, and my whole body tingled as his fingers engulfed my hand. I watched as he slid the ring that he'd kept for me all these years onto my finger. My heart swelled with love for this man and ached for all the pain he must have been carrying for so long. The fact that he still loved me after what I did and what my mother did, made me realize that I was never going to find another man like Jax.

He was my person. He was my everything. And I was determined to spend the rest of my life proving that to him.

He lifted up my hand and pressed his lips to the ring. I watched him, allowing myself to feel the love that I'd stifled for all these years.

When he finally dropped my hand and met my gaze, I reached up and pulled him in for another kiss. We were going to spend the evening making up for lost time. There was never going to be another moment when I was without him or he was without me.

Jax was my person, and I was never, *ever* going to let him go again.

And tonight, I was going to show him just how deeply I meant the three little words, *I love you.*

18

CLAIRE

SWEET TEA &
SOUTHERN GENTLEMAN

S unlight spilled into Jax's room. My eyes fluttered open, and a smile crept across my lips as I took in the warm morning glow. I closed my eyes and focused on the soft, rhythmic sound of Jax's heartbeat against my ear.

I was snuggled against him, feeling the warmth of his body as it cascaded down mine. My hand was sprawled across his chest as if it were trying to touch as much of his body as possible. His arm was wrapped protectively around me like the last thing he wanted to do was let me go.

This was heaven. My thumb found the ring he'd slid onto my finger. I twisted the band around, wondering what it meant. Did he propose? Were we engaged?

We didn't do much talking last night. My body was sore but alive at the same time. So much had changed between us, and yet, there were parts that were similar. I smiled as I remembered asking him if his lips felt the same.

He shifted under me, and I tipped my head back to see him glance down at me. I smiled, and he smiled as he settled back onto his pillow. He tightened his grip on me as he drew me closer to his chest.

"Morning," he murmured before pressing his lips to the top of my head.

"Morning," I replied, running my hand up and down his chest. He didn't respond at first, but a few seconds later, his other hand reached up and wrapped around mine to still it.

"What are you doing to me, woman?" he growled before lifting my hand and kissing my fingertips.

I giggled and pushed up onto my free hand, my hair cascading down my shoulder. I swung my leg over his waist, and as soon as the weight of my body settled on him, his eyes sprung open, and his gaze met mine. Fire burned inside of it, igniting my own desire.

He moved to sit up, but I pressed my hands to his chest to keep him still. He growled in frustration, but I just shook my head.

"We need to talk first," I said with a giggle.

Jax's hands went to my waist before he slipped them down to cup my rear. "Talking is so overrated."

I pressed down once more on his chest, my gaze dipping to the ring on my finger. I sucked in my breath before raising the hand and wiggling the ring in his face. "I need to know what this means," I whispered.

His gaze dipped to the ring before he brought it back up to me. "What do you mean?"

I swatted his chest. "It's a ring, Jax. What does it mean?"

He studied me before he reached up and engulfed my hand in his. "What do you want it to mean?"

That was not the answer I wanted to hear. I wanted a man who knew what he wanted. If it was me, he needed to say it. I scoffed as I climbed off his lap. My feet landed firmly on the floor.

"Claire," he said as he scrambled to follow me.

I padded across the floor to his bathroom, but he stopped me before I could get there. His hands found my waist, and he spun me around to face him.

"Is this going to be a habit of yours? Running away so I have to chase you?"

I glared at him in a playful way. "Are you going to keep saying stupid things?"

"Asking what you want the ring to mean was stupid?"

I nodded. "Idiotic." I glanced down at his chest. "I want to know what *you* want it to mean. What do *you* want from me?"

His expression stilled as he studied me. The air between us changed as he stepped closer. The want between us intensified as he stared down at me.

"I want you to be my wife." His hand found my cheek before he slipped his fingers through my hair. "I want you to be the mother of my children. I want to grow old with you, forever." His lips brushed mine. "And I never want to watch you walk away again."

I smiled against his lips, centimeters from mine. "Are you sure?" I whispered.

He didn't answer. Instead, his lips crashed into mine, and in that moment, I knew the answer. His pounding heart beat in time with mine.

He was mine, and I was his. Nothing and no one would ever come between us again.

I would love Jax until the day I died. And from the way he stared at me, from the way he touched me, I knew he felt the same.

"I'M JUST SO HAPPY," Rose's voice cracked. She kept glancing between me and Jax as we drove her to her house.

She was sitting in the front seat of Jax's truck while Jax drove. I sat in the back with my hand wrapped around the seat, so Rose could hold it. She kept twisting my ring around my finger before kissing it and setting it back down.

"I just knew you two kids would get together. You are meant for each other."

Jax grinned as he glanced at me in his rearview mirror.

"And now a wedding! I'm so blessed."

I smiled over at her. "We're just glad you're here to see it." I steeled my expression. "No more emergency surgeries. No more scares. Do you understand?"

Rose nodded. "No more hospitals. I'm done with that."

I smiled, even though the memory of her lying on the ground ashen and limp would haunt me forever.

"I'm just grateful to be going home."

I patted her shoulder. "We all are."

Jax pulled into her driveway and got as close to her front door as he could. Rose let go of my hand, and I climbed out of the truck just as Jax rounded the hood, so he could help Rose down. We worked together, Jax helping Rose while I carried her things into her house. Her daughter was just a half hour away from arriving, so we helped her get settled.

She was sitting in her lounge chair when there was a knock on the door. "That must be Ysabel," Rose said as she sat up straighter in her chair.

"I'll get it," I said as I stood. I held out my hand to stop Rose from moving. She shifted but, thankfully, didn't try to get up.

I walked over to the front door and pulled it open. The narrowed eyes and pursed lips of my mother were the last things I expected to see. She let out a sigh as she glanced past me into the room.

"I thought you'd be gone by now," she said, her tone curt.

I swallowed my frustration and stepped to the side. "We're waiting for Ysabel and then we'll go."

Mom stepped into the entryway, but just before she moved to walk past me, she stopped. "We?"

I swore in my mind when I realized what I'd just done.

But before I could answer Mom's questions, Jax appeared in the doorway between the living room and the kitchen. Mom's gaze snapped to him before she sighed and glared down at me.

Rose spoke first. "Missy, let's—"

"I see where your loyalties lie," Mom snapped, interrupting her.

"Missy, why don't you hear her out?" Rose tried again, but my mom wasn't listening.

Her cheeks were bright red, and her gaze burned with disdain as she stared down at me. "You couldn't just stay away, could you?"

"Ms. Hodges." Jax's voice grew louder, and I knew he was coming to rescue, but I could do nothing to acknowledge him. My entire body had frozen under my mother's scrutiny.

Mom snapped her gaze to Jax. "And you. You couldn't leave my family alone. You and your traitorous family. Always finding a way to make me miserable."

Jax's arm wrapped around my shoulder, and all of a sudden, I could breathe again. He was the lifeline I needed, and I could feel his protection as he put himself between me and my mother.

"I don't know what you think you know, but my family never wanted to hurt you. Sure, there was a feud in the past, but we've all but forgotten. You seem to be the only one that can't move on."

Mom sputtered as she glanced from Jax to me. "I'm the

one who hasn't moved on. What about you and your mother? That hussy. She—"

"Enough!" My whole body was shaking now. I was done with my mother. I was done with what she said about me, about Jax, and about Jax's mother. Dad had his freedom. He made a choice, and he chose someone else.

Mom's lips were pressed into a tight line, but she was quiet as she stared at me. I stepped forward causing Jax's arm to drop to his side. I faced my mother head-on as I held her gaze.

"I don't care about the feud. I don't care about how you feel toward Jax. I'm done. Dad was an adult. He made his choice. Whether it was right or not, I'm not going to ruin my life because of something he did."

"But Claire—"

"And I'm done living my life for you. I broke up with Jax when I was a teenager because you manipulated me. I'm not doing that again. I love him. And if you love me, you'll want me to be happy."

Mom's expression tightened like that was the last thing she wanted to do.

"If you can't accept us, then we are over." I stepped back and wrapped my arm around Jax's waist.

She didn't say anything. Her expression was stoic as she stared at me. Her gaze never wavering.

Jax's arm was tight around my shoulders as if he feared I would suddenly change my mind and join my mom. But that temptation was far from my mind.

I glanced up at Jax. His jaw muscles were tight as he stared at her. I squeezed his side, which caused him to look down at me. "Let's go," I said as I nodded toward the door.

He didn't wait. He turned toward the front door and headed outside, calling a soft goodbye to Rose as he went. I lingered for a moment, watching my mom, willing her to care enough about me to put down her petty grievances and be the mother I needed her to be. But her rigid body and pressed lips told me she had no intention of doing that.

She was going to hold onto her grudge like it was the only thing keeping her alive. Even though it was destroying her relationship with her daughter, there was nothing I could say or do that would change her mind.

I glanced over at Rose, who offered me a consolatory smile. I just nodded, acknowledging her support. But I wasn't ready to smile. Not when my relationship with my mother was crumbling in front of me.

I turned and headed toward the door when my entire body just stopped moving. I wasn't done. I was going to speak my piece because it was the only thing I could do.

"I forgive you," I whispered as I turned to face my mother once more.

Her eyes were wide as she stared at me.

"I forgive you because I've seen what a grudge can do to a person. Not finding the strength to forgive has poisoned you to the point of losing everyone who loved you. I forgive you because I don't want to become you. I want a happy, healthy life full of people and experiences." I sucked in my breath in an attempt to hold back my sob. "If you decide to change, I'm willing to see if our relationship can be healed. But until then, we are finished."

Tears began to fall. There was a small part of me that thought it would soften her heart. But it did nothing. She just stood there, staring at me.

Not wanting to stand there, baring my soul anymore, I turned and hurried from the house. Jax was waiting for me outside, and as soon as he saw me, he wrapped his arms around me and pulled me to his chest.

He just let me sob into his t-shirt, not caring that I was soaking it. When I was finally strong enough to pull back, he cradled my head as he stared down at me.

"She doesn't want me," I whispered.

He just shook his head. "She's an idiot."

I loved that he loved me, but it wasn't enough. A person needed a family. They needed a mother, and I hated that my own didn't want me.

"Come on," he whispered, as he wrapped his arm around my shoulder and led me to his truck. He held the door open and helped me into my seat.

I settled in, taking deep breaths to calm my heart. I meant what I'd said to my mom. I did forgive her. There was going to be work involved if she wanted to reinvest in our relationship, but I wasn't going to hold onto a grudge.

I wasn't going to become her.

Jax got into the driver's seat and slammed the door. He started the engine and backed out of Rose's driveway. He straightened the wheels once he was on the road and then glanced over at me.

He gave me a soft smile before he leaned in and pressed his lips to mine. He pulled back slightly and asked me where I wanted to go.

I leaned into him, wrapping my arms around his and laying my head on his shoulder. I took in a deep breath and said, "Let's go get our dog."

19

JUNIPER

SWEET TEA &
SOUTHERN GENTLEMAN

I was angry.

After I shouted at Boone and marched back to Godwin's, I found my parents, and I laid into them. I told them that it was ridiculous that they thought I needed a babysitter. That they way overstepped in their arrangement with Boone—whatever it was. And I told them to their face that I wasn't interested in being managed.

But they didn't care.

Dad told me firmly that they were worried about my safety, and Boone was here to stay. Boone looked like a deer in headlights as he stood behind my parents. This was clearly the last place he wanted to be, but he didn't sprint for the door—which I respected. He did seem like the kind of man who would honor his word. If he told my parents he was going to help—he was going to help. No matter how awkward I made it for him.

Realizing that I wasn't going to get my way, I just grumbled and walked away from the family meeting we were having at the back of the store. I busied myself the rest of the day with checking expiration dates and ignoring texts from Kevin.

Had he not been an idiot and made my parents worry, I wouldn't be in this situation. We'd still be happy together in Texas, and I would be far away from Boone and his bright blue eyes.

I sighed as I stared up at the ceiling. It was the next morning, and I was awake even though I didn't want to be. My stomach was grumbling, and I knew if I didn't eat soon, I was going to get nauseous. That seemed to be happening more and more lately.

I grumbled and pulled my covers off and sat up. I slipped my feet into my slippers and grabbed my robe on my way out of my room. I padded down the hallway and past the doorway that led into the living room. I stopped in my tracks.

Boone was lying on the couch. He was on his back with his hand resting on his chest. His eyes were closed, and his breathing was rhythmic as his hand lifted and lowered with every breath.

I glowered at him, hating that my parents even gave him a place to stay. This was getting out of hand.

Anger pricked against my skin as I made my way into the kitchen. I grabbed a pan and set it down on the stove— probably a bit too loud, but I didn't care. I was upset, and I was going to let the rest of the house know that I was upset.

I went over to the fridge and grabbed out the eggs and bacon. Soon, the classic smell of breakfast filled the room. My mouth was watering as I watched the bacon pop and sizzle. The coffee maker beeped, so I made my way over to pour myself a mug.

"Do you have to be so loud?"

Dad's voice startled me, but I drew my lips into a frown when I glanced in his direction. I was going to be mad for a while. I just glowered at him before taking my coffee over to the stove to keep a watchful eye on my food.

"I'm surprised you're letting me cook my own breakfast. You know, since you think I need a babysitter and everything." I didn't keep my voice low, and I saw Dad's eyes flick in the direction of the living room before he shushed me.

"Juniper, stop," he whispered as he raised his hands and then slowly lowered them. Like that was all it was going to take to get me to comply.

I rolled my eyes and started to take the bacon off the pan and set them on the paper towel next to me. "I can't believe you hired him without asking me."

Dad was in the middle of filling his coffee mug, so it took a moment before he turned to study me. I could see he was chewing on my words as he slowly sipped his coffee. I was blotting the grease off the bacon when he sighed and rested the mug in his other hand.

"Listen, he's a Navy SEAL. He's a little lost, and you

need someone to keep Kevin away. Mom and I figured it would be killing two birds with one stone." His frustrated stare turned to one of desperation as he studied me. "Your mother is worried sick. She doesn't say it, but she stays up at night worrying about you and your safety." He turned his pleading gaze on me. "Would it be so hard for you to just let Boone stick around? At least until Kevin heads back to Texas?"

I took a bite of bacon and chewed, his proposal rolling around in my mind. Thoughts of how Boone came to my rescue yesterday flashed intermittently. The truth was, no, it wasn't going to be hard to let him stick around. Boone was quiet and kept to himself. There were times yesterday that I didn't even notice him around me.

If it was going to give my parents more peace and give Boone something to do while he transitioned back into civilian life, who was I to take the job away from him? I wiped the grease off my fingertips and took another sip of coffee. Then I sighed as I set the mug down onto the counter and folded my arms. "Fine," I whispered.

Dad's eyebrows went up. He parted his lips.

I pointed my forefinger at him before he could speak. "Only until Kevin heads back to Texas. Then all bets are off."

Dad nodded and raised a hand. "I promise."

I didn't like giving in, but if it kept the peace, I would. After all, I doubted that Kevin was going to make Harmony his home for much longer. He always talked about how much he hated the small town. He loved the hustle and bustle of Dallas, and it wouldn't be long before he was missing the city life.

I just needed to keep my distance for a bit longer, and then moving on from my ex would be easy.

I was halfway through my eggs when Boone walked into the kitchen. He kept his gaze low as he asked for a glass of water. Dad showed him where the cups were kept while I shoveled the remaining bits of breakfast into my mouth before dropping my plate into the sink.

I sidestepped them as I headed back to my room to jump into the shower and get ready. Just as I turned off my curling iron, my phone chimed.

I glanced down to see that it was a text from Kevin. I knew I shouldn't pick up my phone, that I should just let it lie, but my resolve faltered. I was curious about what he had to say. Maybe he was telling me that he was leaving Harmony for good.

I swiped my screen on and pressed on the green chat bubble icon.

Kevin: Morning, beautiful. Just checking in to see how you are doing. I hope yesterday didn't make you too upset. I was just excited to see you and worried you'd walk away.

While I was reading, a second message popped up.

Kevin: I guess that's why I held onto your hand so tightly. I just don't want to lose you again. I love you.

My throat went dry as I read his words. I wanted to believe that they were true. I wanted to believe that he cared for me like I cared for him. But this was a road we'd been down so many times before. He'd hurt me and then tell me it was because he loved me. Then he'd say the right thing to get me back and we'd enter this cycle again.

I just wished I had the strength to break things off for good.

I wasn't ready to answer his texts, so I clicked the side button, and the screen went dark. I proceeded to grab my shoes and purse before slipping my phone into my back pocket and heading out to the living room.

The ride to the store was quiet. I could tell Mom was hurt by my reaction yesterday, so I made a mental note to talk to her today. I wasn't ready to forgive her, but I knew living in the same house with her when she was upset was hell. I was ready to put yesterday's conversation behind us.

Dad waited at the back door of the store for us before he unlocked it and stepped inside. Mom assigned me and Boone to continue stocking shelves while she readied the registers. I nodded, grateful for a mind-numbing task to keep the conversation to a minimum. Plus, it was nice to have someone strong who could cart the boxes out to the floor while I stocked the shelves.

We found a groove, and we were down the canned goods aisle when Mom shouted that she was opening the doors for the morning. Boone and I had an assembly line going. I was on the ladder, and he handed me the cans to stock.

When we got to the pearled onions, he handed me a

fresh can, and I glanced down at it. That was a mistake. My stomach flipped at the sight of the cloudy white balls, and the bacon and eggs from this morning decided they were going to make a surprise appearance.

I barely made it down the ladder without falling. I shoved the jar into Boone's hand as I sprinted past him, my hand clasped over my mouth. Luckily, the bathroom wasn't too far away, and I made it just in time.

I was left shaking and weak as I shifted from hunching over the toilet, to sitting on the ground. I'd always been a relatively healthy person growing up. And I'd never in my life thrown up this much without having a fever or some form of heat stroke. These sudden waves of nausea were random and confusing to me.

It was almost like...

My eyes flew open. My heart was pounding. I didn't want to think the words even though they lingered at the edge of my brain ready to jump. I grabbed my phone and found my calendar.

It couldn't be.

I *couldn't* be...

My period was late. In all the hustle and bustle of coming to Harmony and getting away from Kevin, I hadn't noticed that my period was seven days late.

There was a soft knock on the door. I wiped my lips with the back of my hand before I stood and pulled open the door. Boone was standing a few feet off, looking concerned. I didn't think as I grabbed ahold of his shirt and pulled him into the bathroom with me.

His eyes were as wide as saucers as he turned around. His gaze darted around the room as if he didn't know where to look.

"I need you to get me something," I said as I stepped up to him. I was hoping if I sounded confident, he would just comply.

"Okay," he said slowly.

I steeled my nerves as I prepared myself to utter the words I'd never thought I'd say. "I need you to buy a pregnancy test."

He pulled back when my words registered in his mind. He parted his lips like he wanted to speak but wasn't sure what to say.

"You can't buy it here. You have to go to the gas station down the road. And you can't tell my parents what you're doing." I dropped my voice as I whispered, "They would lose their minds."

"Juniper..."

My gaze snapped to him. It was the first time I'd ever heard my name on his lips. I...I didn't hate it.

"I need you to do this." I glanced up at him, meeting his gaze. "Please."

He studied me. I could see his desire to flee race through his eyes, but then he just nodded. "Okay."

He slipped out of the bathroom, leaving me alone. My

mind was racing, and I was doing everything I could to keep my mind free of fear—I was failing.

If I was pregnant, what was I going to do? What did it mean for me and Kevin? He was the father. Did he want to be involved? Was I going to try to make it work?

My stomach lurched again, so I pulled out my phone and distracted myself with movie clips until I heard a soft knock on the door. I stuffed my phone into my back pocket and headed to the door. Boone handed me a brown paper bag. I thanked him and shut the door.

I followed the directions and then set the stick down on a piece of toilet paper on the back of the toilet to wait. I had three minutes to wash my hands and stand on the opposite side of the room, staring at it. Willing it to say negative.

My phone chimed, announcing that the time was up, but I couldn't move my feet. I couldn't read the test. I wasn't ready to make decisions that would forever affect another person's life.

Tears pricked my eyes as I walked toward the door. I prayed that Boone was on the other side. I turned the handle, and when his familiar blue eyes met mine, I waved him into the room. He hesitated but joined me.

Once the door was shut, he turned, his eyebrows raised.

"I can't look," I whispered, nodding toward the test still sitting on the toilet.

Boone followed my gesture with his gaze.

"Will you look for me?"

He parted his lips. He must have seen my desperation

because he closed his lips and nodded. Then he crossed the space between him and the toilet and looked down. The seconds that ticked by felt like millennia. Finally, he glanced up at me. His dark gaze was hard to read.

"What does it say?" I asked, bringing my hands up to my mouth as I braced myself for his answer.

He studied me for a moment before he whispered, "You're pregnant."

20

ELLA

SWEET TEA & SOUTHERN GENTLEMAN

I yawned as I pulled into my parking spot behind Harmony Island Gazette. I'd been up all night writing a piece for Gloria, and I was up way too early with anxiety that I'd written it wrong. I'd gotten a total of about two hours sleep last night, so I was exhausted.

My normal coffee with two sugars wasn't cutting it, even though I'd been nursing the drink on the drive over here. I was going to need an espresso, stat.

I pulled the keys from the ignition and slipped them into my purse. With the strap pulled up onto my shoulder, I opened the driver's door and got out. My phone chimed just as I pulled open the door to the back seat to gather the papers I'd set back there.

I pulled my phone from my purse to see it was a text from Asher. A smile played on my lips as I swiped my phone on, so I could read what he said.

Asher: Have a great day, best friend.

I sent him a smiley face emoji before I stuffed my phone back into my purse. Asher and I had been friends since we were kids. When he moved to Harmony Island as a realtor and discovered that their newspaper was hiring, he told me to apply.

I'd only been in Harmony a short time, but I was loving the small-town vibe. It was exactly what I'd wanted when I decided to become a journalist. Plus, having Asher here made the move that much sweeter.

I leaned forward and grabbed the papers from the back seat, grumbling when I had to bend down to grab a few that had slipped onto the floor. Just as I straightened and stepped back to shut the door behind me, a dark figure moved next to me.

My whole body stiffened as I turned to see a man wearing a black hoodie, with the hood pulled over his head. He was standing a few feet away from me, angling his face so the shadows hid his features.

"Hello?" I asked, my voice wavering as I contemplated dropping my papers to grab the pepper spray in my purse.

"Look into the Proctor family. There's trouble in paradise." And with that, he turned on his heel and hurried away.

I stood there, blinking at his retreating frame. Once he disappeared around the corner, I turned back to my car before glancing back over my shoulder, wondering if I'd just made that entire thing up.

Look into the Proctor family. There's trouble in paradise.

What did that mean?

I frowned as I made my way to the back door of the Gazette. Gloria was somewhere inside, no doubt panicking because my story wasn't here yet. Maybe she had an idea who or what that person was talking about.

I found her in her office with papers spread out all over her desk. One look at me and she crossed the room with her hand extended. I handed her my story, and she took it without so much as a thank you. I lingered against the far wall as she moved around her desk, picking up stories and setting them down.

"A strange thing just happened to me," I said, but my comment only elicited a quick flick of her gaze in my direction. "Some stranger just approached me outside and told me to look into a family in town."

Gloria harrumphed. "Oh yeah? What family is that?"

"The Proctors?"

Gloria stopped moving, and her gaze snapped to me. I pulled back, surprised by her response.

"Is that a bad thing?"

She shook her head. "The Proctors own the paper."

"Okay..." I said slowly. "What does that mean?"

Gloria sighed. "It means the Proctors are off-limits."

***

I hope you've enjoyed reading Godwin's Grocery. I

loved writing Jax and Claire's journey back to love. Even though the road to healing isn't over, I'm glad Claire decided that she was finally going to start living for what she wants... not what her mom wants.

I can't wait for you to dive into Juniper and Boone's romance and introduce you to Ella, the spunky journalist who can't seem to say no.

Make sure you grab the next book in the Sweet Tea and a Southern Gentleman series, The Harmony Island Gazette to find out what happens next!

Wanna a bonus scene between Jax and Claire? Sign up for my newsletter and grab either the SWEET or SPICY bonus scene that fits perfectly right after Chapter 17.

Enjoy!

Godwin's Grocery SPICY scene: HERE or scan below

Godwin's Grocery SWEET scene: HERE or scan below

Want more Red Stiletto Bookclub Romances?? Head on over and grab you next read HERE.

For a full reading order of Anne-Marie's books, you can find them HERE.

Or scan below:

Made in the USA
Monee, IL
12 August 2024

63714780R00152